A HANGING
IN HIDETOWN

A HANGING
IN HIDETOWN

•

Kent Conwell

AVALON BOOKS
NEW YORK

PRINTED IN THE UNITED STATES OF AMERICA
ON ACID-FREE PAPER
BY HADDON CRAFTSMEN, BLOOMSBURG, PENNSYLVANIA

To my Grandfather, Salathiel Dimmitt Conwell,
who told me stories about Hidetown.
I still remember those afternoons on the porch with you, Papa.
How I wish I'd paid more attention.

And to Gayle with all my love.

Chapter One

I grew up in the Shenandoah Valley on a small farm with rich, fertile soil. When I wasn't manhandling a walking plow behind a blue-nosed mule or tending stock, I was hunting in the woods around our place.

Ma died giving me birth. Pa raised me, and he did as good a job as a man could. About once a year, Pa dressed in his Sunday best and headed for his yearly meeting with the local banker. He once told me, "Son, bankers got a wretched way of thinking. A man looks like he needs money, they'll turn away, but let a man look prosperous, and those puffed-up blowhards will scramble all over theyselves to throw their money away."

For the most part, Pa was right. But, he should have

taken his idea one step further to say that "looks were deceiving."

If he had, the two strangers who rode up to our door at the beginning of the War of the Rebellion wouldn't have got the drop on him. But they did, and they killed him right there in the front doorway.

They had their sights on me, but before they got inside the cabin, I dove through a rear window and vanished into the woods. I didn't stop running for two miles. And with every step of those two miles, the picture of their cruel faces burned deeper into my brain.

And since that day, I always looked twice and moved once.

The habit stood me in good stead. I had a knack with a sixgun. I wasn't fast, but I was accurate. I practiced every moment I wasn't working. Within a couple of years, I ran the scavengers down and put a couple of lead plums in their bellies they couldn't digest.

A U.S. Marshal started sniffing at my trail, so I did what any jasper on the run would do. I lost myself in the Great War of the Rebellion. When Lee surrendered at Appomattox, I drifted west, picked up a reputation as a gunfighter, then dropped out of sight.

That's how I came to be sprawled in a patch of scrubby shin oak near the Canadian River up in the Texas Panhandle watching a burly hombre back-shoot another in a murder that would change the rest of my life.

The wrist-thick trunks of the shin oak grew so close together, I could see only a slice of the drama unfolding. Other cowpokes, spurs jingling and chaps rustling, moved in and out of my line of sight.

Abruptly, the shooter turned and stared in my direction. He had a square jaw and deep-set eyes under a protruding forehead. I held my breath. I knew he couldn't see me, but my muscles stiffened just the same. My fingers closed around the butt of my .44.

Gesturing with his still-smoking handgun, he yelled, "Let's ride, boys. The buzzards can take care of W.T." They headed east along the river.

Earlier, I had camped in a gully over the hill and was heading for the river to fill my canteen when I spotted the riders coming up the river. That was when I scooted into the patch of shoulder-high shin oak.

During the war, bitter experience taught me not to camp by a body of water unless I could see in every direction. And once again, the lesson paid off.

After the last hoofbeat faded away, I counted to five hundred, slowly. And just as slowly, I peered over the top of the shin oak.

Shucking my Navy Colt, I eased over to the dead man. About thirty or so, I guessed. He looked like an owlhoot, rode hard and put away wet. I studied the lay of the prairie around me. Just the hot sun and the sagebrush waving in the ever-present wind. In the distance, a red-tailed hawk was pinned to the blue sky.

With the prairie wind blowing in my face, I studied the dead man for several seconds. I felt no regret for him. He probably got what he deserved, but what of his family? In the years to come, they would always wonder about him. For them, I did feel regret and sorrow.

Glancing around again, I quickly knelt and searched him for some identification. He had a plug of Red Moon tobacco with a single bite missing, a bag of Bull Durham, and a worn Barlow knife, all of which I returned to his pockets. His killers had taken his guns and boots. "Sorry, pard," I whispered, rising to my feet.

I glanced at the tracks in the soft soil. A bright glitter caught my eye. I picked it up and studied it. The object was a piece of silver shaped like the state of Texas with a hole in the middle. I puzzled over it a moment before realizing it was the rowel of a spur. I peered in the direction the gang had disappeared. Probably one of the owlhoot's.

My first impulse was to drop it in my vest pocket, but on second thought, I tossed it back on the ground. I wanted nothing to connect me with this incident. I had enough trouble without asking for more.

I studied the tracks left by the ponies. I shook my head when I spotted one with two missing nails. "You won't go too far, friend," I muttered, holstering my

Colt and hurrying back to my camp. I wished I could have buried him, but I couldn't afford to leave any evidence of my passing.

Five minutes later, I was riding due south, away from the river. Later I would cut southeast for Hidetown where I was to meet Obery Phillips and pick up my wages for the broncs I had busted up in Atascosa.

What I should have done was continue southwest into the Staked Plains. That vast expanse, treeless and burned brown by the blistering summer sun, would have been a tropical oasis compared to the trouble that would fall on me in Hidetown.

Chapter Two

The white quartz sand comprising the rolling hills of the Texas Panhandle easily tires both man and horse. Several times during the day, I pulled up for a breather, loosening my pony's cinch.

The sun's glare off the sand was almost too intense for the eyes, forcing me to squint. Slowly, I made my way across the hills and rugged gullies until I reached the headwaters of Sweetwater Creek, a pristine stream that twisted across forty miles of Texas Panhandle into Indian Territory to the east. The darting shadows of fat bass and sassy bluegills zigzagged beneath the clear water.

A knoll rose above the stream, shaded by ancient cottonwoods. From the rise, a jasper could see for miles. I noted a worn road beyond the stream, but decided to still take advantage of this campsite for the night. Best I could figure, Hidetown was only an hour or so away. I could ride in fresh the next morning.

I caught a couple of bass, split them down the middle, and spitted them to broil above a small fire. The crackle and pop of the sizzling fillets made my mouth water.

Suddenly, the clatter of a wagon and the jangling of trace chains sounded from the prairie behind me. I leaped to my feet and ducked behind a cottonwood, Colt in hand.

From around a distant sandhill, a buckboard with two figures on the seat bounced into sight. I saw immediately they were youngsters. I remained behind the tree as the clattering wagon drew near.

Without warning, a back wheel separated from the wagon, sending the rear axle digging into the sand and the butcher blade wheel bouncing into a shallow gully cut by rain.

The girl screamed, but the boy held tight to the reins, pulling in the startled horse. The girl squealed again.

"Hush up, Emmabelle," the boy shouted. "We're all right."

She hesitated, her mouth open. "You sure, Danny?" She looked around from her perch on the seat.

Danny wrapped the reins about the brake handle. He removed his battered felt hat and wiped his sleeve across his forehead. He appeared to be around twelve or so—Emmabelle two or three years younger. "Sure, I'm sure."

He tugged his hat back on his head of black curls and shuffled through the sand to retrieve the wheel. "You're going to have to get back here and help me."

She brushed her hand over her hair and gave Danny a look of exaggerated disdain. "I'll get all dirty."

He jammed his fists in his hips. "So what? I can't put the wheel back on by myself. If you don't help me, we'll have to walk into town. Then you'll really be dirty."

Holstering my sixgun, I stepped from behind the tree. "Need a hand, kids?"

Danny jerked around in surprise. His eyes cut toward the Winchester on the seat of the buckboard. I held up my hands. "I don't mean any trouble, boy. I'm camped over here."

Emmabelle gaped at me, her eyes wide.

Slowly, Danny eased toward the Winchester. I grinned and stepped back to prove I meant them no harm. "You need a strong back to lift the wagon."

He eyed me warily.

"When we finish," I added, "you're welcome to share supper with me." I nodded to the fire. "Fresh fish."

He hesitated, studying me. Finally, a broad grin erased the frown on his face. "Thanks, mister. I'm Danny Ryan. This here's my sister, Emmabelle. We'd be obliged for your help."

"Call me Jace."

Emmabelle just stared at me. I nodded to her as I sloshed across the stream. She continued to stare.

Luckily, the accident had not damaged the wheel. We slipped it back on the axle. Danny looked up at me in disgust. "I lost the blasted nuts," he said, referring to the hub nut and lock nut.

"Just use the lock nut from another wheel, but don't forget to replace them when you get to town."

Emmabelle had not moved.

I gestured across the creek to my camp. "Hungry?"

She glanced at Danny, who nodded. A tiny grin magically appeared on her face. "Sure am."

They made short work of the fish.

The sun was nearing the horizon. "You youngsters are welcome to spend the night."

Danny shook his head. "Thanks, mister, but we got to get on to Hidetown." He nodded to Emmabelle. "We're supposed to spend the night with our uncle and aunt. They'll be worried if we're not there by dark."

I leaned back against my saddle. "Well, you take care. How far is it on in to Hidetown?"

He shrugged his narrow shoulders. "Not far. Four, maybe five miles. Just follow the creek. It runs right down beside the town."

I watched as the buckboard disappeared around a bend in the road. Far to the north, a wolf howled.

*   *   *

I'd met Obery Phillips in a poker game in Plaza Atascosa near the New Mexican border where he hired me to break a dozen mustangs. One, a grulla, almost broke me, but I finally smoothed that gotch-eared hammerhead. When I finished polishing off the rest of the broncs and went looking for my pay, I discovered Obery had left town, leaving me a few dollars and instructions to meet him in Hidetown.

To be perfectly honest, I figured he had snookered me on the mustang deal, but I wanted to give him the benefit of the doubt before I stomped him into a grease spot.

As I rode out of town, I spotted a hombre who looked strangely familiar. He stared at me, but I kept riding. That night, I lay awake trying to place him. He reminded me of a jasper I had killed in a gunfight years ago. Maybe he was kin.

To be on the safe side, I rolled out of my soogan, ate a hasty breakfast, and rode out before the sun. Just in case someone was behind me.

Seemed like running was all I had done since those two scavengers chased me out of our cabin years before.

On the southern end of the Jones and Plummer Trail to Dodge City, Hidetown was a trading center for buffalo hide and various freight. The village lived up to its name, for most buildings were constructed of buffalo hides and sticks. Trees did not grow in abundance in the Texas Panhandle, making the import of building materials necessary. And wagonloads of building materials were few and far between because of the Comanche terror across the Panhandle.

Most structures were therefore a hodge-podge of whatever materials were available, with the exception of a few wooden buildings—the general store, all four saloons, the sheriff's office, a two-story hotel, the livery, and the gallows at the edge of town, from which dangled an unlucky cowpoke covered with buzzing flies.

Obery wasn't in town so I did what any self-respecting cowpoke would do, I took a spot at the bar in the Buffalo Horn Saloon. The way I figured, when Obery hit town, first thing he would do would be to wash the trail dust from his throat.

If I didn't find him here, I'd try another saloon. Sooner or later, I'd run across him in one. If he'd cut out on me, I'd still find him. Besides my knack with a sixgun, I knew how to track people.

To my relief, he hadn't tried to double-cross me. I found him about mid-afternoon when I ambled into the Alhambra Saloon. Skinners and hiders jammed the saloon, their buckskins caked black with grease and reeking of putrid meat. Laughing women in garish makeup escorted drunken cowpokes to the second floor.

I spotted Obery at a table in the middle of the room. He held up his glass when he spotted me. He was covered with a thick layer of dust that billowed from his sleeves each time he moved an arm.

"I was thirsty," he laughed. "Been dirty so long, I reckoned I could tolerate it a mite longer until I got some whiskey down my gullet."

I grinned back at him as I sat. "Don't reckon I'm much better. Washed up some at the creek last night." I downed a slug of whiskey fast in a hopeless effort to allay the stink of the room.

He drained his glass and refilled. "No creek for me. I'm going for a hot bath and bed at the hotel. Soon as I pick up our pay for the mustangs from Sam Nelson, I'm going to spring myself to a shave, haircut, hot bath, and a new set of duds." He slapped at his vest. "These are just worn thin as a sheet of Bull Durham."

I laughed. "Sounds right appealing to me. When's Nelson due in?"

"About sundown." Obery must have noticed the frown on my face. "Problem?"

Glancing around the saloon, I grunted. "Not so to be something to worry about." That was a lie. As far as I knew, that cowpoke back in Plaza Atascosa could have put the law on my tail.

"You hard up for cash?"

I grinned sheepishly. "Reckon so." I patted my empty vest pockets. "I wouldn't mind one of those hot baths."

He fished a few crumpled bills from his pocket.

"Here. Take this. On account. Soon as Sam comes in, I'll hunt you down."

"Much obliged, Obery. If I'm not in town, I'll be camped back west, on the creek."

I wished I'd had enough coins for clean duds. Kind of defeats the purpose, donning dirty clothes after a hot bath, but a jasper can't be too particular, especially out in the middle of nowhere like the Texas Panhandle.

I can't blame anyone but myself for what happened that night. If I had eaten more and drank less, I wouldn't have been so sleepy as not to hear the soft scratch of footsteps in the sand.

But I didn't hear them, nor did I feel the blow to the back of my head that knocked me out.

But I sure enough felt the rough hands that jerked me awake.

I blinked against the morning sun and tried to rub the sleep from my eyes, but claw-like fingers held my arms to my side. I managed to croak out, "What's going on here?" I struggled against the clutching hands.

"Shut up, you saddle tramp," a voice shouted. I glanced at a lantern-jawed jasper just as he swung the back of his hand at my jaw, knocking my head around. Stars exploded in my head, and my ears rang.

Adrenaline surged through my veins. With a Herculean effort, I swung my arms forward, jerking the hombres holding me off balance and slamming them into each other. I grabbed for my handgun, but the muzzle of a sixgun jabbed me hard in the small of the back.

"One move and you've bought six feet of dirt, cowboy."

I froze. I was wide awake now.

Half-a-dozen men stood with drawn sidearms, glaring at me. Four of them wore badges. A red-headed badge-toter nodded to the figure wearing a red plaid shirt sprawled on the ground by the ashes of my campfire. A blood-stained hole was in the middle of his back. "You're going to hang for this, cowboy."

My brain was beginning to function. Hang? I remembered the poor soul stretching a rope back in Hidetown. "For what? I didn't shoot him. I don't even know him."

"That's a lie," another hombre replied, stepping through the cluster of steely-eyed lawmen. He looked more like a businessman than a gunsel. He wore a collarless boiled shirt and linen trousers. "I saw you two in the saloon together yesterday."

"Not me." I shook my head.

The first deputy cut his eyes toward the rail-thin hombre who had spoken. "You certain about that, Cletus?"

Cletus nodded emphatically. "Sure as hogs root, Burgess."

I shook my head. "That's a lie. I don't know this jasper."

A bald-headed deputy stepped forward and rolled the dead man over with the toe of his boot.

I gaped. Obery Phillips!

My jaw dropped open even wider when I saw Obery's spurs. One rowel was missing. The other was silver, shaped like the state of Texas.

Chapter Three

The jail cell in the sheriff's office was a cramped room with a snubbing post sunk in the middle of the floor to which one end of a heavy chain was attached. On the other end of the chain was an iron cuff, which they promptly locked around my ankle.

Cletus Jackson turned to the bald-headed, fat deputy. "You, Gotrain. Where's Meechum?" he snapped impatiently.

Gotrain scratched his protruding belly. "The sheriff ought to be here. We sent word."

The iron cuff bit into my ankle despite my boot. "Listen to me, all of you. I didn't kill Phillips. Why should I? He owed me for breaking some broncs."

One of the deputies, Joe Carstairs, sneered. "You

probably kilt him and hid the money." He narrowed his eyes. "I reckon I can beat the truth out of you."

Jackson stepped forward. He glared at Carstairs. "There won't be no beatings around here, deputy. The law will take care of this." He paused, his eyes burning into Carstairs's. "If Meechum won't stop you, I will."

A deputy with a crooked nose sneered. "Stay out of this, Jackson. We'll handle it."

Jackson shot the deputy a chilling look. "You don't take care of nothing, Halliburton, except keeping the law." He glared at the deputies. "You understand?"

An older hombre with a weather-beaten face stepped up beside Jackson. "He's right, Halliburton. The law will take care of this."

The deputy eyed the second man in disgust. "What's it to you, Perkins? This jasper is pure trouble."

The door swung open and Sheriff Jack Meechum strode in.

I froze when I saw the protruding forehead over the face covered by five days of beard. He was the same jasper I witnessed shoot the old boy on the Canadian River the day before.

Groaning inwardly, I felt myself sinking deeper and deeper into the quicksand of futility. The sheriff was a cold-blooded killer, and one of his henchmen—Obery Phillips—was found dead in my camp.

Deputy Carstairs filled Meechum in on the events of the morning. When he finished, the sheriff turned to me. I searched his eyes for a sign of recognition, but to my relief there was none.

"Well, cowboy, looks like you got yourself into a heap of trouble."

"Look, like I told them, I—"

"I know what you told them. What I want to know is what you did with the money you took from Phillips."

I glanced at the faces looking at me. "I didn't take any money."

"You're telling me you didn't even search him after you killed him?"

"No. You're confusing things. I didn't kill him. I didn't see any money."

Halliburton snorted. "Let me beat it out of him, sheriff."

I drew back, doubling my own fists. They had me chained like a bear to a post, but I could still do some damage before they got me.

"That's enough, Meechum," Jackson said, pushing through the deputies. "I've told your boys once, this is going to be handled by the rule of law. You understand?"

Meechum shrugged his broad shoulders and scratched at the rough beard on his broad jaw. "Well now, Jackson. We got us a cut-and-dried situation here. You saw the two of them together, and this morning we find this Obery Phillips in this hombre's camp, deader than old Abe Lincoln. I don't see much sense in wasting time and money for a trial when the verdict will come down to the same rope anyway."

Obviously, Jackson carried some weight in Hidetown. I addressed him. "Sure, I knew Obery, Mister Jackson. He hired me to bust some broncs up at Atascosa, then follow him down here to get paid. That's all I know." I laid my hand on the back of my head. "Here. Feel this. Someone put this knot on the back of my head last night. Next thing I knew, you old boys was jerking me awake."

Jackson eyed me suspiciously. "What's your name, cowboy?"

"Quinlan." I glanced at Meechum who was eyeballing me like he would take delight in stomping me into the ground. "Jace Quinlan. I drifted down from Santa Fe, looking for work. I met Phillips at a poker game in Plaza Atascosa. And . . . well, I told you the rest. Last I seen of him was when I left the Alhambra Saloon late yesterday."

Meechum snorted. "You believe that trough of pig slop, Jackson, and you got feathers for brains. I tell you what happened. Quinlan here spotted Phillips carrying a heap of greenbacks. He invited him out to the camp and killed him. Hid the money."

I shook my head. "No. Phillips was just about as broke as me. He was waiting for Sam Nelson to come in and pay us."

"Mighty convenient," Carstairs said.

"Check with Nelson."

The deputy grunted. "That's what I meant by convenient. Nelson rode out last night."

I was growing desperate. "Go get him."

Jackson started to speak, but Meechum spoke up. "Now listen to me, Cletus. Carstairs has got a point. I run into Phillips out on the road yesterday about noon. He was packing a bundle of greenbacks in a money belt under that bright red plaid shirt of his."

Jackson eyed Meechum suspiciously. "Then where's the money?"

Meechum shrugged. "Quinlan there hid it."

Jackson looked at me.

I shook my head. "I didn't do it, Mister Jackson. I can't prove it, but I didn't kill Obery Phillips."

Later that day, a younger deputy brought me a tin plate of beans and bread. The beans were cold, and the bread was hard, but they tasted like Christmas dinner. The young deputy handed me a cup of water and stepped back. He watched silently.

When I finished the plate, he took it. "You want some more, Mister Quinlan?"

His demeanor surprised me. I suppose he saw the surprise on my face, for a sheepish grin played over his lips. "We're not all like the others."

For the first time in several hours, I grinned. "Thanks. What's your name?"

He shrugged his shoulder and in a shy voice replied, "Bud. Bud Tunney. The sheriff is my uncle. He raised me after my folks was kilt by the Cheyenne." He glanced at the door. "Uncle Jack, he's tougher than a whetstone. Had to be."

Before I could reply, a porky man in a linen suit and unbuttoned vest opened the door. He was short, so short he looked like someone had cut him off at the knees. "Where's your uncle, Bud?"

The young man shrugged. "Out and about somewhere, Mister Potter."

Potter shifted his gaze from the young deputy to me. "This the hombre what killed that other jasper?"

Bud glanced at me. "That's what they say."

Potter pulled a red bandanna from his hip pocket and blew his nose. He lowered his voice. "Best keep an eye out, Bud. Word is that jasper won't see the sun come up in the morning. There's talk of giving him a dose of hemp fever. They done took the other one down and buried him."

The young deputy glanced around at me, his eyes wide, his mouth gaping. He recovered quickly and shook his head. "Don't you worry none, Mister Quinlan. They ain't going to hang you. They gotta go through me first."

If the circumstances had been a little different, I might have smiled at his youthful determination. But, given the situation facing me, I didn't have the inclination for even a tiny grin.

Throughout early afternoon, Hidetown boomed with trade. Wagons rattled in loaded with buffalo hides;

curses from the skinners and hiders echoed above the clanking of chains; cattle bellowed in the corrals; frightened horses snorted; and drunken cowboys shouted as they staggered from the saloons.

The remainder of the day dragged by. I paid no attention to the young deputy who jabbered incessantly, constantly reassuring me that he would protect me if a crowd gathered.

I came up with an idea, not much of one, but it was all I could figure. And I needed a couple breaks for it to happen.

The sun dropped below the western horizon. Bud Tunney removed the chimney from the coal oil lantern and wiped off the buildup of black soot before lighting the lantern. The yellow flame filled the dark jail with dim, dancing shadows and the acrid stench of the burning coal oil.

It was time.

"Hey, Bud." He looked up. I nodded out the window in the direction of the outhouse. "I need to make a visit."

With the naïve innocence of youth, he nodded and fished the key from the sheriff's desk. He tossed them to me, at the same time drawing his handgun. "Just don't try nothing."

Nodding at the Colt in his hand, I replied. "Don't worry. You're holding a mighty convincing argument there."

He grinned and relaxed.

I tossed him the keys and rose to my feet, stretching my arms over my head. "Feels good," I said. I pointed to the door behind him. "Somebody to see you."

"Huh?" He glanced around. "Hey," he exclaimed, turning back to me. "There's no one . . ."

I moved quickly, slamming a straight right into the point of his chin. He dropped like a tow sack of corn seed. I grabbed his shoulders so he wouldn't slam his head against the floor.

Hastily, I grabbed my gunbelt from the peg on the wall and strapped it on, at the same time moving to the back door. I opened it a crack and peered up and down the alley. Night shadows poured in between the houses. To the west, the last pink of the setting sun slipped below the black line of the horizon.

I ducked into the nearest shadow, letting my eyes grow accustomed to the darkness. I glanced back at the dim light glowing through the window of the jail. I had to hurry. The young deputy would be coming around any moment.

The clamor and clatter of wagons and horses and drunken men echoed up and down the street, covering what little noise I made. My only fear was to run into someone who might recognize me.

I scurried through the shadows from shack to shack. Once, a mongrel dog bared his teeth and snapped at me. I kicked him in the head, sending him yelping into the night.

Abruptly, the back door of one of the buildings opened and a man stuck his head out and yelled at the dog. "Shut up, you mangy critter, or I'll serve you for supper tonight."

I dropped into a crouch just around the corner from him, so close I could smell the grease on his clothes. He stunk worse than a line rider's longjohns.

He picked up an object and hurled it into the night. The cur dog yelped and went skittering into the darkness.

Muttering under his breath, the hombre stomped back inside and slammed the door. A shout came from the direction of the jail. The young deputy must have come around. I hurried on down the alley.

Pausing near the edge of town, I stood in the shadows of a clapboard building and stared out over the prairie. Wide open and beckoning, it offered a false sanctuary, for come morning, I would be out there like a fly in the middle of a sugar pile, a fly with busted wings.

To my right was the main street. Ponies were tied to the hitching rails. It would be a small matter to swing onto one and race out of town, but the streets were too crowded with laughing, shouting cowpokes and buffalo skinners. Someone would spot me.

No, I reckoned my best bet was to spend the night in town, in the anonymity of a crowd, but where? The livery? That's the first place they'd look.

A grin ticked up the edge of my lips. I knew the

perfect place. The barber shop—the tonsorial parlor with the $1 beds that Obery Phillips had mentioned. If it were like most, the beds were pallets on the floor in a room that would accommodate thirty or forty snoozing hombres.

I tugged my hat down over my eyes and eased toward the street, stumbling and staggering like I was drunk. I paused at the hitching rail, playing the part of a soused cowpoke. My fingers quickly untied a couple reins, which I left dangling from the rail.

Hiccupping, I staggered across the street and into the parlor. Keeping my eyes lowered, I wobbled to a stop in front of a mustachioed attendant who was absorbed in a dime novel, and forked over a wadded greenback. He jammed a flea-ridden blanket in my hands, and I stumbled into the sleeping quarters.

A dozen figures slumbered on the floor. I found a pallet against the canvas wall so if worse came to worse, I could slip out easily.

I lay where I could watch the door. Between the fleas, the constant clamor of rowdy cowpokes, tinny pianos, laughing crib girls, and waiting for the sheriff to come bursting in, the time passed slower than a three-legged turtle.

Chapter Four

The noxious vapors of unwashed bodies, stale beer, sour whiskey, and greasy buckskins filled the room with a suffocating odor that clogged my nostrils. But that was the least of my worries.

I kept my eyes on the door and my ears tuned to the streets.

I didn't have to wait long.

Within minutes, I heard shouts up and down the one street of Hidetown. I tightened my grip on my revolver. I hoped I wouldn't have to use it. For over five years, I had run from the reputation I made after the war. Folks had forgotten me or thought I was dead. I was still nervous over that jasper back in Atascosa.

The uncertainty, the worry, the running—that was the price for youthful foolishness and stupidity.

More voices joined in the shouting.

I lay motionless, feigning sleep, snoring lightly.

Suddenly, the blocky figure of Sheriff Jack Meechum filled the doorway. He stood motionless, staring at us.

I eased the muzzle of my Colt around until it was centered in the middle of his chest. To my regret, I was in too deep to try to wound a jasper. I had to shoot for my own life.

Just as he took a step into the room, one of his deputies rushed in, shouting, "Sheriff! He stole a horse. A cowpoke from the Bar V claimed someone stole his horse."

Meechum spun. "He see Quinlan?"

The deputy hesitated. "He's a mite drunk, sheriff, but he claims he spotted Quinlan heading north out of town, toward the Canadian."

The sheriff jammed his handgun in his holster and bolted from the parlor. I gave a sigh of relief and relaxed, until another flea started biting me.

After the hoofbeats of the posse faded into the night, I rolled under the canvas wall into the darkness. Now was my chance to light a shuck out of Hidetown. I wondered about my own pony. Chances were, it was down at the livery. I couldn't risk stealing it back.

I crouched in the shadows between the general store and the Buffalo Gal Saloon, studying the street. The batwing doors of the saloon swung open and two men came out. "You and Halliburton take the south end of town. I'll take the north. Don't let no one out and check every wagon. Jack ain't sure, but he don't want to take no chances in case that jasper's trying to pull a slick one."

I grimaced and muttered a silent curse. Meechum was no one's fool.

Staying on the balls of my feet, I turned back to the alley. I needed a safe haven to consider my next move. I found what I was looking for beneath the back porch of Cletus Jackson's home. Of course, I didn't know it was Jackson's at the time. That was a stroke of luck, and the good ears of a young boy were my next stoke of luck.

Jackson's house sat on piers. He had enclosed the open space beneath the clapboard structure. Under the porch, he stored various items in wooden boxes, which I quickly discovered I could move together and create a hidey-hole for me from anyone peering through the tiny entrance.

Just after sunrise, the deputies came, searching all homes.

After scouring Jackson's house, they paused by the small door under the porch. "What's under there?"

I recognized the voice of Deputy Carstairs.

Then little Danny Ryan's voice chirped up. "Nothing, sir. Mister Jackson just has some junk in boxes."

"Junk, huh? Well, let's take a look."

I tightened my finger on the trigger of my revolver and stared at the line of light around the small door forming a rectangle.

The door opened slowly, emitting a faint glow into the crawlway.

Danny replied. "Go right on in, mister, but be careful. I killed a rattlesnake in there yesterday. Uncle Cletus says there's probably a nest under there."

The door stopped abruptly. "What was that?"

"Rattlesnakes. There might be a nest under there."

Abruptly the door slammed shut.

I looked over my shoulder into the darkness, unable to believe I had crawled in with a nest of rattlesnakes. My heart thudded in my chest, and my throat grew dry as a drought.

I sniffed the air. Rattlesnakes, most snakes, have an odor. Unfortunately for me, it is similar to the musty smell under a house, except a tad muskier.

The deputies left, but I was too concerned with my own predicament to hear them. Next thing I knew, someone was rapping on the porch over my head.

I jumped like I'd been snakebit.

Then Danny's voice came down through the cracks. "Jace? You hear me?"

My brain reeled in confusion. How the blazes did he know I was under here?

"Jace?" His voice grew louder.

I looked around frantically. "Hush," I whispered back. "You'll stir up the snakes."

He giggled. "There ain't no snakes under there. I just told the deputy that so he wouldn't crawl under."

Well, a wagonload of worry slid off my shoulders. Before I could question the boy, he continued. "I was up early this morning when you snuck under there. You best stay put. They're looking everywhere. I'll fetch you some biscuits directly."

"I don't have time, Danny. I've got to get out of town and fast."

He remained silent a few seconds. "Listen, Emmabelle and me are taking supplies back to our ranch this morning. The buckboard is by the side of the house. Crawl under the canvas, and I'll stack our supplies on top of you."

I didn't have a choice. "All right, here I come."

"No. Not this way. Crawl under the house. There's another door on that side of the house. It opens close to the buckboard."

Under the house? I peered into the darkness. "Danny?"

"Yes, sir?"

"You sure about those snakes?"

He laughed softly. "Honest. I just made that up, Jace. But, watch out for centipedes. We killed a big black and red one in the house last night. I figure they come from under there."

Centipedes! He might as well have said rattlesnakes as far as I was concerned. They both scared the blazes out of me.

He pressed his lips to the crack and whispered. "You hear me?"

"Yes. Okay." I holstered my sixgun and pulled my collar up about my neck. I started crawling. My skin tingled like I'd picked up a dose of lightning.

The tiny cracks around the trim permitted just enough light for me to make out the ground in front of my hands. Once, a toad frog popped up. I stifled a shout, but banged my head on a floor joist when I jerked back. I grimaced, hoping no one above heard me.

I continued crawling, my breath coming in raw gasps.

Suddenly, a snake slithered in front of me, only inches from my outstretched hands. I froze, anticipating the burning strike of fangs, but to my relief, nothing happened. I could hear the soft scritch-scritch of the snake's belly as it wound it way into the darkness.

I crawled a lot faster then. Moments later, I pushed open the small door and scrambled under the canvas, not realizing my clothes were soaked with sweat and my heart was beating faster than a hurdy-gurdy gal can hustle a drink.

Minutes later, the house door slammed and I heard Danny say. "Yes, ma'am, Aunt Martha. We need to get back. Jenny'll be worried." He quickly hitched the team and then climbed up in the wagon and began rearranging the supplies, covering me completely.

The front door squeaked open. A woman's voice said, "Next time, Danny, have Jenny come with you. I worry about her out there by herself."

"I'll try, Aunt Martha, but no need to worry about her. She can outshoot most men. Besides, old Watts and Tevis is there."

Concern edged her voice. "But they're old men."

Danny laughed. "Yes, ma'am, but they sure got some good stories to tell. Better'n we hear in church."

"Danny!" Aunt Martha exclaimed in shock.

He laughed again. "Just joshing, Aunt Martha. Just joshing. Old Watts, he reads to us from the Bible every day. No need to be concerned about us."

"Well, at least he does that."

Emmabelle shouted. "You ready, Danny?"

"Climb in, Emmy. Let's go."

"Don't call me Emmy."

The springs in the seat over my head squeaked as the youngsters plopped down. Danny popped the reins. "Let's go, Joe, Buck. Gee-haw."

A deputy stopped us at the end of the street, but when he recognized Danny and Emmabelle, he waved them on through.

The buckboard was rough and jarring. Dust billowed up through the cracks. Danny didn't stop until we reached the site of my camp two nights earlier.

Emmabelle said. "What are you stopping for, Danny?"

"Need to water the horses—and take care of some business."

"What kind of business?"

"You'll see," he replied, climbing into the bed of the wagon and moving some of the supplies. "You okay, Jace?"

I wormed out from under the canvas and dusted myself off. "Reckon so." I recognized where we were. Then I nodded to Emmabelle who was staring at me in disbelief. "Morning," I said with a grin.

She looked up at Danny. "What's he doing here?"

"I'll explain later," Danny said, handing me an oil-skin package and a canteen. "There's them biscuits and bacon I told you about. Reckon you're hungry now."

"I reckon so," I replied, settling back in the wagon bed and taking a long drink of water. "How far to your place?"

"Not far. Two hours or so." He popped the reins and the wagon clattered on down the road.

"Think I can get a loan of a horse?"

He hesitated. "Reckon we can find one. We lost some a while back to rustlers."

I remembered the owlhoots I had spotted back on the Canadian where Meechum plugged one in the back. "Rustlers? Lose much stock?"

"I ain't real sure, but Jenny worries a heap about it."

Emmabelle tugged at Danny's sleeve. "Is Jace going to work for us?"

"Naw." The young boy chuckled. "We just helping out a friend who shared his supper with us, that's all."

"Oh." Apparently, his explanation satisfied her for she turned around a smiled at me. "Jenny is a good cook. Maybe she'll be frying steak tonight."

I winked at her. "I'd like that."

As we approached the ranch house, a slight figure appeared in the door and stared at us.

"That's Jenny," Danny volunteered.

"Her name is Jennifer," Emmabelle said primly. "Jennifer Louise Ryan. She's our cousin."

As soon as I had a good look at Jenny Ryan, I knew she possessed that brand of tenacity and boldness the West demanded of its women. Whatever jasper she consented to marry could consider himself mighty lucky.

She strode out to meet the wagon. The hot wind tousled her short brown hair, and her teeth contrasted sharply with her sun-darkened complexion.

Danny introduced us. She eyed me warily, her misgiving obvious. "He helped us fix the wagon and then gave us supper," Danny explained.

Without a trace of a smile, she nodded. "Much obliged, Mister Quinlan. You're welcome to spend *a* night."

I didn't miss her emphasis.

"He needs to borrow a horse, Jenny," Danny added, giving me a worried glance.

For a moment, she hesitated, then smiled at Danny. "That's fine." She cupped her hand to her lips and cried out. "Tevis!"

An old man limped to the open door of the barn. "Yes, ma'am."

"You and Old Watts come help with the wagon."

He nodded and shuffled toward us.

Jenny stretched out her hand to Emmabelle. She spoke over her shoulder to us. "Supper's almost ready. You men come on in when the wagon is unloaded."

Old Watts and Tevis joined us at the supper table. The fare was simple but filling—steak, succotash, biscuits, red-eye gravy, and hot coffee for the grownups and milk for the youngsters.

Throughout the meal, I managed to dodge or evade most of the innocent questions Old Watts and Tevis asked of me, but I couldn't help noticing that Jenny kept giving me curious looks.

After the meal, we dumped our dishes in a pan of boiling water. I looked around for a dishrag and towel.

Jenny said. "Looking for something?"

I grinned at her. "Thought I might wash up the dishes to repay some of your kindness, ma'am."

For a moment, she appeared taken aback, but she quickly recovered. "Why, thank you, Mister Quinlan, but that really isn't necessary. That job belongs to Emmabelle. You probably need your rest tonight since you have to leave so early in the morning."

I grinned inwardly at her subtle, but clear suggestion. "I reckon you're right about that, ma'am."

I couldn't sleep. I didn't cotton to the idea of running from something I didn't do, but Meechum had the cards stacked against me back in Hidetown. Only an idiot or fool would play against that kind of hand. On the other hand, I'd been running for years. Once more wouldn't mean a heap in the grand scheme of things.

I rose and wandered outside. The stars filled the heavens, so thick in places you couldn't see the black of the sky. I rolled a cigarette and leaned against a hitching rail.

"Something on your mind?" Jenny's voice startled me.

"Huh?" I looked around in surprise.

"I just asked if there was something on your mind."

"Oh. No. No." I relaxed. "I was just noticing what a nice little place you have here."

She took a step closer and gazed around the ranch. "It's been a lot of work."

"Two nice kids too."

She laughed softly. "That's been a lot of work too."

I chuckled. "Reckon so." I paused, took a drag on the cigarette, and blew the smoke into the night sky. "I appreciate you putting me up and for the loan of a horse. I'll pay you back."

She shrugged. "Don't bother."

"No, I will." I hesitated again. "I like those kids of yours. You've been gracious, though I know you will be right glad to see the back of me. Regardless, I feel like I need to be honest with you. Whatever you might hear about me, well, it isn't true. Back in Hidetown, they say I killed a man. I didn't. All I'm guilty of is getting drunk. I broke out of the jail, and now I'm on the run." I took another drag on the cigarette.

After a moment, she said. "Why are you telling me this?"

With a shrug, I replied. "You seem to be a good person, Miss Jenny. You and the kids. My pa taught me to never tell a lie. I admit that's caused me some problems along the way, but on the other hand, I never had to remember made-up stories. That's why I wanted to shoot square with you."

A fetching smile played over her face. "That's decent of you, Mister Quinlan, but for your information, I already knew about you."

I gaped at her in surprise. "About me? But—"

"The sheriff was out here. He told me what took place."

For a moment, I digested her answer. "And you're still making me the loan of a horse?"

She looked up at me. "I don't know if you're guilty or not. All I know is you helped my little cousins and gave them something to eat. You can't be all bad. So, in the morning, take one of the horses and leave."

I studied her a moment. "Thanks."

"And take one of the good ones. If I know Jack Meechum, you'll have to do a heap of riding to get away from him."

Chapter Five

I rode out before sunup on an iron gray gelding, deep-chested and long-legged. With a bag of grub tied behind the saddle and a canteen of water dangling from the saddle horn, I planned to ride across No Man's Land up into Kansas. Once in Dodge, maybe I'd turn west for California.

Having spent my earlier years in wooded country, the boundless panorama of the undulating prairie had a hypnotic effect. I'd catch myself gazing in the distance, my thoughts marveling at the wonder around me. I could see how the vast, open spaces of the Panhandle could intimidate a jasper until he came to terms with it.

Mid-morning, I pulled up in a motte of shady cottonwood around a small spring for a breather. A hot wind blew across the rolling prairie, cooling my sweat-soaked shirt.

I glanced at the tracks around the tiny spring. Others had visited it recently. I climbed off the gray pony and patted his neck. "Drink up, boy. We're wasting time." I removed my hat, enjoying the breeze drying the perspiration on my forehead while studying the most recent hoofprints in the damp sand.

Something about them was familiar. I frowned and squatted, lightly tracing around the outline of the shoe with my finger. There were two horseshoe nails missing. Suddenly, I realized I had seen the shoe before, on the Canadian River. There was a shoeprint there with two missing nails.

What were the chances of another horse missing the same two nails on the same shoe? Slim and none. Yep, the hombre who made these was with that band of back-shooters I had spied upon four days earlier.

I rose quickly, searching the rolling hills around me. I looked back at the tracks. They headed north, the same direction I was traveling.

"Maybe I should just head for Colorado," I muttered, climbing back into the saddle and turning northwest. I'd skirt Atascosa to the east, the jasper with the two missing horseshoe nails to the west, and head straight for Denver.

Fifteen minutes later, I reined up, studying a cloud of dust directly ahead of me.

I tied the gray to a sagebush and on my belly

squirmed to the top of a sandhill. To the north, several cowpokes were pushing a herd of beeves and horses east. I blinked. Even at this distance, some of the horses looked familiar. Then I recognized the grulla that had almost broke me up in Atascosa. I studied the other ponies, picking out a sorrel and a pinto.

Those were the mustangs I had broken for Obery Phillips. I shook my head slowly, wondering if that horse thief had me busting stolen cayuses.

Of course, I couldn't know for certain they were stolen, but given the fact he ran with outlaws didn't speak any too well for his innocence. Truth was, while I had no hard proof the herd had been rustled, the evidence sure pointed in that direction.

On the horizon beyond the herd, the rolling hills ended at the base of the caprock, a vertical cliff above which stretched the Staked Plains, flat and treeless from horizon to horizon, nothing to serve as a landmark.

The early Spanish explorers called it the Llano Estacado, the staked plains, for they were forced to drive stakes in the ground to find their way back to their camps.

As I lay there under the blistering sun, the herd disappeared behind a sandhill. I waited for it to reappear beyond the hill, but ten minutes later when it had not, I grew curious.

Mounting my gray, I rode to the next hill and dismounted, tying my horse to a slender oak. I crawled to the top of the hill.

The herd had turned north, heading for the caprock.

I followed for about an hour until they pushed the herd into a narrow ravine that opened into a great canyon. There was no sign of a ranch house or corrals. After the last animal entered the canyon, two cowpokes placed wood rails across the entrance.

I released a deep breath. If I'd ever seen a rustlers' holding pen, this was one.

A rider on a yellow dun pulled out and headed east. He wore a black shirt.

I studied the situation, guessing I had discovered where they hid their stolen plunder.

A wild idea took hold of me. If that jasper back in Atascosa had recognized me and called in a U.S. Marshal, maybe I could find a way to use the marshal to bring Meechum to ground, and clear myself at the same time.

Hurrying back to my gray, I cut east, angling northward until I could pick up the cowpoke on the yellow dun.

He traveled hard, crossing into Indian Territory just before sundown. He made a cold camp. I followed suit.

Next morning, I followed him another twenty miles until he rode into Fort Reedstrom, a major outpost on the western side of Indian Territory.

I watched from the shade of a tree-lined creek not

far from the fort. It appeared Meechum had a nice little game going for himself. As sheriff of Hidetown, he was above suspicion. He and his gang rustled stock, drove it across the Panhandle, and sold it to the army, probably at prices double the going value.

I kept my eyes on the gates to the fort, waiting for the reappearance of the yellow dun while I tried to formulate a plan of some sort.

But who would believe me?

I thought of Cletus Jackson, the Ryans' uncle. He didn't take any guff from Meechum, and I had the feeling he wasn't any too keen on the sheriff.

But how could I convince him?

At that moment, the cowpoke in the black shirt rode out of the gate on the yellow dun. I studied them a moment.

Suddenly, I knew how to convince Jackson. I had my answer. I banged the heel of my hand against my forehead. "Why didn't I think of that before? That'll do it. That'll convince him."

Obery's shirt, the red plaid shirt Meechum claimed he saw Obery wearing; the one under which Meechum claimed he saw the money belt. That shirt was my bargaining tool.

I was so excited, I started talking to the gelding. "Meechum couldn't have seen Obery in the red plaid shirt. Phillips was still in his old clothes in the saloon at sundown. Why—"

The words froze in my throat. My head reeled with conjecture.

That meant Meechum saw Obery after I left, after Obery cleaned up and donned his new duds. "Which means Meechum couldn't have seen Obery around noon wearing the plaid shirt," I muttered. "And, I'll give ten-to-one odds that Meechum back-shot Obery just like he did that jasper back at the Canadian River."

Why?

I shrugged. No telling. Obery was in Meechum's gang. Maybe there was a falling-out. Maybe Obery wanted more money or maybe just decided he'd had enough of the outlaw game.

And me, I just happened to be at the wrong place at the wrong time. That's why I got the blame.

The rider on the yellow dun crossed the creek a quarter of a mile north of me and headed back to Texas.

Retrieving my sack of Bull Durham, I rolled a cigarette and watched until the yellow horse disappeared over the horizon. I dismounted and stretched my legs. I was in no hurry. I knew where the rider was heading. What I had to do now was figure out how I could get to Cletus Jackson for his help.

Desperate times call for desperate measures, and as far as I was concerned, these were desperate times, and I was desperate. I was wanted for murder, was maybe even being pursued by a marshal, and I was completely on my own.

I peered to the north. Maybe I should just ride on out. Maybe the idea of giving Meechum his just desserts and clearing myself was nothing more than a wild dream.

But I knew I was going to try. At least, I was going to take one stab at it. I couldn't live with myself if I didn't.

I wasn't crazy about going back into Hidetown, but I had no choice. I waited until dark to approach the village. The rattle of the tinny pianos and laughter from the saloons drifted across the prairie, somehow making me feel even more alone. I tied my pony to some sage and slipped in after dark.

A faint light glowed from a window in Jackson's home.

Moving silently, I crouched beneath the window and peered into the room through the tiny parting of the curtains. Cletus Jackson sat at a rolltop desk, poring over a set of accounting books.

His wife, wearing a bonnet and shawl, nodded to him and gestured to the door. I grinned to myself. She was leaving the house.

I slipped up to the front corner of the house and waited. Moments later, she stepped onto the porch and descended the steps. I remained in the shadows as she headed down the boardwalk toward another building into which several women were entering.

Shucking my sixgun, I hurried up the porch and

opened the door. From the parlor came Jackson's voice. "What did you forget now, Martha?"

Quickly, I stepped into the parlor and centered the muzzle of my Navy Colt on him. "Hold it right there, Jackson."

He blinked in surprise, and then his eyes grew wide when he recognized me. "It's you. The killer. Quinney."

"Quinlan, and I'm not a killer."

He reached for a drawer in the desk.

"Don't try it. I'm not here to hurt you."

Jackson glared at me. "That handgun says different."

I studied the slender man a moment. "Let's just say, for the moment I feel more comfortable with it in my hand."

He narrowed his eyes in suspicion. "What do you want?"

"Talk. That's all. Just talk. Then I'll leave."

"All right. Talk. I got work to do."

"If I remember right, you say you saw me and Obery Phillips in the Alhambra Saloon the other day."

"That I did," he replied, his pointed chin jutting in determination. "You can't deny that either."

"I'm not trying. Now, I want you to stop and think. Sheriff Meechum said he saw Phillips earlier that day, about noon. Phillips was wearing a red plaid shirt. The reason Meechum remembered it was red plaid was because he claimed Phillips showed him the money belt underneath it. You remember?"

A puzzled frown erased the suspicion from his face. "Yeah. I remember Meechum saying that. So what?"

"Just this. When I was with Phillips in the saloon at sundown, when you saw us, he still had on his trail duds. He told me he was going over to the tonsorial parlor for a shave, a bath, and a set of new clothes. If you saw me with him, then you know he wasn't wearing the red plaid."

Jackson gazed through me as he replayed that afternoon over in his head. An expression of disbelief filled his face. "No. No, you're right. He wasn't wearing the red shirt. He had on a dirty vest and an old cotton shirt so bleached by the sun it was almost white." He frowned at me. "What does that mean?"

I took a step closer. "It means Meechum saw him after you and me, not in the middle of the day. Why would Meechum lie about seeing him earlier in the day? What would he have to gain? Unless he didn't want anyone to know he had seen Phillips after we did? I think Jack Meechum had a hand in Obery Phillips' death. That's the only way he could have seen the red shirt."

Jackson's eyes narrowed. "What about the money belt? Where's it at?"

"Maybe he didn't have one." I shook my head. "At least as far as I know. He had a few wadded-up greenbacks in his pocket. He was waiting for Sam Nelson to ride in and pay him for the mustangs I broke. He might have gotten the money belt from Nelson."

Jackson leaned back and studied me. "I ain't fond of Meechum. I always suspected he might bend the law some. Blazes, out here, most jaspers bend the law. But killing? That takes a heap of believing."

I took another step closer and holstered my Colt. "What if I tell you I saw Meechem back-shoot a jasper a few days ago up on the Canadian River?"

He arched an eyebrow. "I reckon it's easy to accuse someone who ain't here."

With a chuckle, I nodded. "Yeah. This hombre was named W.T. That's all I know."

Jackson stiffened slightly. "W.T.? You said W.T.?"

"Yep. No last name. When Meechum holstered his gun, he told his gang to ride out. 'Leave W.T. to the buzzards,' he said."

A puzzled frown knit his forehead. "There was a jasper here for a few days by the handle of W.T. Trevor. Drifter, I figured. He rode out. Figured he was heading up to Dodge or thereabouts."

"And that isn't all. One of the gang lost the rowel to his spur, a rowel in the shape of the state of Texas. You go look at the spurs on Obery Phillips, and you'll see he is missing a rowel just like that."

Jackson remained silent a moment, studying the matter. "Phillips has done been planted, but I reckon the undertaker might have noticed."

"You want proof I'm telling the truth, you can find

that other rowel up on the Canadian with the remains of that W.T. hombre."

Jackson rose and massaged the back of his neck with his hands. "That's a mighty hard story to believe."

I figured I had nothing to lose by telling him about the herd, the mustangs, and the ride to Fort Reedstrom.

The angular man plopped down in his chair. He ran his bony fingers through his thinning hair. "If this is all true, Meechum is a thief, a rustler, and a murderer."

"I can even show you where they're holding the herd back north of here."

He looked around at me, a new respect in his eyes. "You say Phillips was part of the gang?"

"Yes." I nodded emphatically. "See for yourself. Talk to the undertaker. Ask him about the spurs."

For a moment, he debated, then nodded. "You wait here. I come back, and you're gone, I'm going straight to the sheriff."

A surge of exultation rushed through my veins. "I'll wait. Don't you worry."

I accompanied him to the door. "Remember," Jackson said, tugging on his hat, "wait here."

From the shadows of the foyer, I peered out the window, hoping his wife wouldn't return first.

A few minutes later, Jackson emerged from the undertaker's. In the middle of the street, he hailed Sheriff Jackson. They spoke a moment, then both headed in my direction.

Chapter Six

Blast that Cletus Jackson!

He double-crossed me. I muttered a string of curses as I shucked my sixgun and backed into a dark corner of the foyer. I glanced toward the rear of the house. If I hurried, I could make it out the back and across the prairie before they opened the door.

I glanced one last time out the window and hesitated. Jackson and Meechum had stopped at the edge of the dirt street. The sheriff was peering to the south in the direction Jackson was pointing. With a nod, Meechum turned on his heel and headed back to his office.

Jackson looked after him, then ascended the steps.

I remained in the shadows, wary as to just what Jackson was up to.

50

He closed the door behind him and entered the foyer. He paused and looked around the room.

"Here I am." I stepped from the shadows, the Colt still in my hand.

"What the—" He spun around in surprise and jumped back when he spotted the handgun pointed at him. He laughed nervously. "You scared me out of ten years' growth."

I gestured to the street with the muzzle of my handgun. "What was all that palavering with the sheriff out there?"

A conspiratorial grin played over his lips. "I told him that a rider from one of the ranches had spotted a band of rustlers working back south, pushing stolen beeves to Atascosa." He nodded to the window. "If I'm not mistaken, Sheriff Meechum and his deputies should be riding out anytime now."

Sure enough, when I peered out the window, Meechum and four deputies were slapping leather to their ponies. But I was still suspicious of Jackson. "What did you do that for?"

He raised an eyebrow. "I don't know whether to believe you or not, but I'll give you a chance. You said you could show me where the rustlers are holding stolen cattle. Well, I want to see it. And on the slim chance you might be right, I didn't want Meechum to wonder about where I was heading, so I sent him off on a wild goose chase."

I studied him a moment, then holstered my Colt. "I'll meet you north of town."

We met up a mile or so out of town and headed a little west of north. Because the rolling prairie looked much the same in one spot as another, I figured the simplest plan was to cut the cattle trail and follow it to the box canyon.

The stars lit the prairie with a bluish glow, casting sagebrush in dark relief against the white sand. I suppressed a nagging fear that the cattle would be gone. After all, the jasper on the yellow dun had time to reach the box canyon and push the herd out immediately.

That's what any smart man would do, but I had always held the belief that rustlers and smart were as uncommon to each other as brogans on a dance hall girl. No, I was counting on them being as dumb as dirt and lazy as a blue tick hound with a full belly.

We crossed the Canadian well before sunrise and continued north. We rode without speaking. Come false dawn, I pulled up.

"This the spot?" Jackson's voice sounded sort of thin and brittle in the vastness of the Texas prairie.

"Not sure. All these hills look pretty much the same," I replied, studying the sandy ground around us. "Our best bet is to keep in the same direction. Once we find the trail, then we'll follow it on to the canyon."

Jackson grunted. We rode slowly north.

Just as the sun peeked over the horizon, we found the trail. "Here it is," I said, reining up. The wind had smoothed the sand some, but the cow patties were fresh enough to assure me that this was the one I had watched a couple days earlier.

Back to the north, the caprock spread from horizon to horizon.

We rode east. Fifteen minutes later, I spotted a patch of oak shinnery on the side of a sandhill. "That's it up there. I tied my horse to one of the oaks," I said, keeping my voice low. "The canyon is north of us, another hour or so."

An hour later, we reined up. "The canyon is just beyond that sandhill.

Jackson pushed his hat to the back of his head and dragged his sleeve across his forehead. "Well, let's us take a look."

I grinned crookedly. "Why not? We can tie our ponies to the sage and crawl to the top where you can get an eyeful."

Jackson got an eyeful.

"Son-of-a-gun," he muttered when he spotted the milling stock in the canyon.

We were lying on our bellies, resting on our elbows. He looked around at me. "Now, understand something, Quinlan. I'm as jealous of Meechum's innocence as I was of yours. I see cows out there, and I'll admit it looks like a dandy spot to hold a stolen herd, but that don't prove Meechum did it."

I studied him a moment. "You're a fair man, Jackson. That's why I come to you. I wouldn't want to put the blame on no man unless he deserves it. Why—"

"Look!" Jackson interrupted me and pointed to the entrance to the box canyon. "Ain't that Halliburton? Meechum's deputy?"

I squinted. "Reckon so. I recognize that crooked nose of his."

Jackson chuckled. "He always looked like he was trying to smell his right ear."

Keeping my eyes on the deputy, I whispered. "So, now what?"

He grunted. "I want to see that other rowel, the one that matches the one Obery Phillips was wearing."

A rush of impatience hardened my voice. "That could give them time to escape, Jackson."

He eyed me levelly, his own voice firm and clipped. "They won't escape, not with the herd. I'm some convinced, but like the cowpoke said at the breakfast table, 'I want some more molasses on my flapjacks. I want to make sure the taste is just right.' " He peered to the west. "How far you reckon it is to that spot on the Canadian?"

I glanced over the prairie. "Like I said, I'm not familiar with this neck of the woods, but I'd guess we could reach it by sundown. I'd reckon it was a dozen or so hours from Hidetown."

*   *   *

The putrid smell of rotting flesh reached out to us when we were still a hundred yards from the bend in the river. I closed my throat to the suffocating odor.

"You was sure right about old W.T.," Jackson said, pulling his kerchief over his nose.

W.T.'s body was not in the small clearing, but the sign was easy to read. Animals had dragged it away. A heavy pocket of stench emanated from north of the clearing. I guessed that was where the remains lay.

Fighting back the reflexive gagging in my throat, I studied the ground. The almost-constant wind had covered the banks with a veneer of sand. I feared that the rowel had been covered. Back to the east, night rolled toward us.

I dismounted and using the toe of my boot, scraped the sand in the area where I had dropped the rowel. Jackson was at my side.

Suddenly, he exclaimed, "Here it is." He squatted and scooped up a silver object. He held it up.

A smug grin played over my lips. "What did I tell you?"

He nodded, studying the rowel. "This proves that Obery Phillips was here, but it doesn't prove Meechum is a rustler or killer."

My patience snapped. "You saying I'm making all this up? That I'm lying?"

He cut his eyes at me sharply, surprise freezing the grin on his face. "No. No. I'm just saying that we need more proof. I believe you Quinlan, but understand, you're a stranger. We don't know nothing about you. Not yet. We need more proof." He dropped the rowel in a vest pocket. "We need to catch him red-handed."

For several seconds, we stared at each other. "I can tell you how," I said.

A frown knit his brow. "How?"

"Remember when I told you about Fort Reed-strom?"

Like the sun rising on a spring morning, the frown faded from his forehead, and a small grin ticked up the edges of his lips. "He's got to take the herd to the fort."

I nodded.

"And we'll be waiting for them."

"I reckon that would be proof enough." I arched an eyebrow.

Jackson nodded briefly. "If he don't have a legal bill of sale for the stock, it will be proof enough to send Meechum to Huntsville Prison for a mighty long spell."

"Can you get enough townfolk to ride with you? You can figure Meechum'll have at least five or six owlhoots with him."

The dark of the prairie night flowed around us. I couldn't see the expression on his face, but Jackson's voice echoed his determination. "I'll get the help, don't worry."

The iron gray gelding I rode was growing weary.

He was about used up. "I'll pick up another pony and meet you at the creek outside the fort."

We kept our ponies in a running two-step. "I meant to ask you about that gelding. He looks familiar."

"Should be. Your niece made me a loan of him."

"My niece?" He looked around at me. Even in the faint starlight, I could see the confusion on his face.

"Jenny. Jenny Ryan."

He shook his head. "Jenny ain't my niece."

"But Danny called your wife Aunt Martha."

A grin replaced the confusion. "Danny, huh? No. We ain't kin, but we've knowed them youngsters for years. They just like family. That's why the gelding looked familiar. How'd you come to meet up with them?"

I danced around the truth, not wanting to cause the youngsters any trouble. "I helped Danny fix his buckboard, and then when I had need of a horse, well, Miss Jenny offered me one. I figure she just wanted me out and away so I wouldn't be an unseemly influence on the kids."

Jackson laughed. "She is touchy about the kids. Treats them just like they was her own."

"Where's their folks?"

"Comanche killed Jenny's back in Sixty-eight or nine. She went to live with the kids' folks, her uncle and aunt, but they caught the smallpox and died a couple years later. Jenny and the youngsters, they been running the place since with the help of Tevis and Old Watts."

He fell silent. I was glad. I didn't want to tell him I was planning on riding back to the Circle R to beg Jenny Ryan for a swap.

I rode into the Circle R around four o'clock. Everyone was sleeping, even the mongrel dog and the rooster. Unsaddling the gray, I turned him loose in the corral. I was exhausted. My eyes were closing when I climbed up in the hayloft, and I don't even remember putting my head down on the hay.

Voices awakened me about mid-morning. My eyes popped open, but I lay motionless, trying to figure out the location of the voices.

At first, they were indistinct murmurs, but as I swept aside the cobwebs of sleep, they became more distinct. They were coming from the other end of the barn.

I recognized Jenny's voice, and chills ran down my spine when I heard the harsh, guttural rasp of Sheriff Jack Meechum. "Just you keep your eyes open, Jenny. That jasper is a killer. He's still around somewhere. Just don't go helping him none."

Jenny replied in an off-hand manner. "You know better than that, sheriff. I won't do anything against the law."

Meechum's tone grew beseeching. "Why do you

keep calling me sheriff, Jenny? Why don't you call me Jack?"

"Why, sheriff, that isn't proper. Not with you being our law and all."

"But, I thought that maybe, after all this time that, well, we might be a little more friendly to each other."

For some reason, a touch of jealousy stirred my blood. I rolled over and peered through the straw at the couple standing in the open doorway. My heart flip-flopped when I saw her brushing the gray I had brought in only hours earlier.

Her voice grew serious. "I told you, sheriff. I have responsibilities here. I can't think about myself. There's Danny and Emmabelle. You know how Danny feels about you."

Meechum's voice grew harsh. "He'll learn. I'll make sure he learns."

Even in the shadows of the barn, I saw the consternation on her face. "He just needs time, Jack. That's all."

His demeanor changed abruptly when she called him by his given name. "I suppose you're right. I just don't like waiting."

At that moment, a horseman appeared on the hard-pan beyond the couple. The sun silhouetted the rider. "We're ready, sheriff."

Meechum muttered a curse, then slapped his hat on

his head. "I'll be back later," he growled, "soon as I take care of business."

Jenny smiled, nodded, and went back to brushing the gray.

After the last hoofbeats died away, she called out. "All right, Jace Quinlan. You can come out now. They're gone."

Chapter Seven

Her voice startled a sparrow perched on a roof joist.
It fluttered in a circle for a few seconds until it spotted
the open door. I felt the same way, confused, surprised, even startled.

I peered through the hay. She was brushing the
gray's mane. Sliding backwards, I clambered down the
ladder and glanced outside. "You sure?"

"Yes." She continued grooming the gray.

I had planned on revealing to her everything Jackson and I had discovered, but after overhearing the
exchange between her and Meechum, I decided to use
a little discretion. "I'm obliged to you, Miss Jenny."

Without looking at me, she said, "I figured you were
smart enough to be out of the state."

She was a fine-looking young woman, much too

good for someone like Jack Meechum. I wondered why she couldn't see him for what he was. I shoved the thought from my mind. "I planned to, but then I hated to run from something I didn't do." I continued, telling her what I had shown Jackson, but I was careful to not mention his nor the sheriff's name.

Folding her arms across her chest, she eyed me skeptically. "I don't suppose you have a witness to any of this."

"One. He's lining up a posse." I paused and glanced in the direction Meechum had disappeared. "That's why I'm back here, to swap the gray for another pony." I hesitated. "With your permission, naturally."

"Who is it? The witness, I mean."

"Jace!" Danny Ryan raced across the hardpan toward us. "You're back." His face glowed with excitement.

Jenny shook her head. Her short brown hair bobbed up and down. "He's just trading horses, Danny. You run back inside and rustle up a bag of grub for Mister Quinlan."

I grinned at her, secretly grateful for Danny's timely interruption. "Thanks."

Immediately, I grabbed a rope from a peg on the wall, swung out a loop, and placed it over the neck of a sorrel gelding. "Nice animals you have here, Miss Jenny."

"You never did tell me who your witness is, Mister Quinlan."

Slipping the bridle on the gelding's head, I kept my eyes averted from hers. "No, ma'am. If I'm wrong about the guilty party, I don't want no trouble for him."

Danny came sliding to a halt, a bag of victuals in his hand.

I felt her eyes on my back as I saddled the pony and tied the grub to the cantle.

"You coming back, Jace?" Danny asked.

My eyes met Jenny's. There was something in them, but I couldn't figure out what. "Sometime, boy." I swung into the saddle and patted the sorrel's neck. "You folks made me loan of this pony. I'll return him."

I headed east, reaching Fort Reedstrom at sundown. A search of the saloons and various businesses turned up no evidence of Jackson and his posse arriving ahead of me. I made camp alongside the small stream outside the fort.

I laid a small fire in a scooped-out hollow to hide its glow. I awakened at every rustle of leaves, random voice, or hooting of an owl. By early morning, I began to figure that Jackson had changed his mind once he got back to Hidetown.

Two hours after sunrise, a small herd of cattle and horses topped the rolling hills to the west and headed along the worn trail to the fort. I watched from the shadows of the cottonwoods as Meechum and his band of rustlers pushed the stock into the corrals outside the fort.

Meechum handed the army officer a sheath of papers. Bills of sale, I guessed. The officer perused them, nodded, and counted out a stack of greenbacks.

I was still watching when the rustlers disappeared over the rolling hills back into Texas. A frown wrinkled my forehead as I wondered what happened to Jackson.

Tightening the cinch, I swung into my saddle and headed back to the fort. I wanted a look at the brands on the stock. Even without Jackson, I could begin building me some proof of Meechum's guilt.

A detail of soldiers was moving the stock. I pulled up and nodded to a corporal supervising the detail. "Looks like you got some fat beeves and frisky ponies there," I said.

The corporal grunted. "Looks that way." He looked up at me. "You got business here, cowboy?"

"Nope." I shook my head. "Just passing through. Thought I'd stop and watch."

He laughed bitterly. "Wish I was just passing through this godforsaken place."

I stiffened. A few of the horses had Circle R brands. I eyed the beef. Circle R there also. There were about forty beeves and a dozen ponies.

After a couple more minutes, I waved to the corporal. "Take care, you hear." I rode into the fort where I picked up a few supplies at the sutlers. I borrowed the storeowner's pencil and on the brown paper he had used to wrap my grub, I drew the brands I remembered. The were four—the Circle R, Cross T, Bar N, and BBB.

By the time I rode back out, the detail had finished its job and departed. I angled past the corrals, searching for different brands, but I failed to spot any others.

I paused at the creek. Staring down at the cold remains of my fire, I pondered my next move. To the north was new country where a jasper could start all over. "Until," I muttered, "someone from the past rides in."

A bitter laugh rolled out of my throat. When was I going to face the fact that there was no running from the past? The past is the only real truth. The future is simply a maybe that can be altered by the slightest gust of wind or fragment from the past.

With a click of my tongue, I turned west, for Hidetown and a confrontation with my past.

A mile out of Hidetown, I pulled behind a sandhill as a shadowy rider raced past. I waited until he was out of sight before moving.

Hidetown was its usual clamorous self, raucous, rowdy, and unruly.

I tied the gelding behind a hill east of the noisy town and slipped in, hiding in the shadows of Jackson's house. Staying in a crouch, I eased forward to a lighted window.

Inside were half-a-dozen ladies dressed in their Sunday best, all attempting to soothe a distraught woman sobbing in a wingback chair. Then I noticed the black bow in the window above my head.

My blood ran cold.

Jackson?

Through an open door to an adjacent room beyond the crying woman, I spotted a casket. Viewers stood contemplating the deceased, then moved into the next room and paused beside the red-eyed woman. Each leaned forward, whispered in her ear, then moved on as her grief began anew.

Staying on tiptoe, I eased to the front of the house, hoping to pick up some information.

I tried to convince myself it was not Jackson in the casket, the one man who believed my story.

The front door opened. I ducked deep into the shadows. A couple departed, the man holding his wife's elbow as they descended the front steps.

"Poor Martha," the woman whispered. "What's she going to do now?"

Her husband replied, "I suppose run the store just like Cletus did."

I closed my eyes and sagged to the ground, leaning against the side of the house and dropping my chin to my chest. My worst fears had been realized.

Cletus Jackson was dead!

* * *

I don't know how long I sat there in the darkness, all hollow inside. Slowly, my numbed brain began to function. Jackson was my only hope. As much as I wanted to stay and clear my name, I'd be foolish to make the effort now.

As much as I hated to admit it, my best chance now was to run.

Without a backward glance, I headed back to the prairie, careful to stay in the shadows. Once out of town, I dropped into a crouch and dodged from sagebush to sagebush.

Behind me, laughter and gunfire echoed across the prairie.

As I slipped around the base of the hill behind which I had tied my horse, he whinnied. I grimaced. If anyone heard him, they might come to investigate. But I reminded myself that with all the clamor in Hidetown, chances were no one would even hear a mule bray.

I reached to untie the reins from a sage.

A hard voice froze me. "Hold it right there. Don't even flinch."

I held it. "Easy, partner. Easy." My brain raced. I couldn't go back to jail. The mob would hang me before the night was over.

"Now, just you put them hands over your head and turn around."

"You bet." I slowly lifted my hands and turned to face him. A lanky hombre, he was too far to reach in one lunge, but I had no choice. I had to take a chance.

Chapter Eight

If I had been surprised earlier when the lanky jasper got the drop on me, I was even more surprised when he lowered his sixgun and said, "I thought it was you, Quinlan."

"Huh?" That was all I could say.

He holstered his revolver. "I'm Bert Perkins. I own the livery. I was with the bunch when they caught you and stuck you in jail."

"But what—"

He glanced around and shook his head. "There ain't no time to talk. Jackson got back-shot. Meechum claims it was a wild slug some drunk fired off down at the saloon. And the story stuck."

"How did Meechum find out about Jackson?"

Perkins shook his head. "Beats me. He figures you

was behind Jackson. He ain't certain, but he suspects mighty hard. We got to get you someplace where you'll be safe."

I didn't know whether to believe Perkins or not. "Where you got in mind?"

He reached for the reins. "My livery. Right under their noses."

I pulled the reins away from him. "You're taking a risky chance on my life, aren't you?"

He snorted. "Not as risky if you head out across the prairie. Meechum sent half-a-dozen deputies out to look for you not more'n thirty minutes ago."

I remember the shadowy rider earlier on the road. A shiver ran up my backbone.

Perkins sensed my reluctance. "We ain't got a heap of time, but Jackson told me what you showed him. He told me about the red shirt. I was there. I remember that just like Cletus did. I just never thought about it." He paused and glanced over his shoulder. "Let's go now. Just walk between me and the horse. Nobody will pay us no attention."

I figured I had about as much chance as a cricket in a chicken yard, but we passed down the crowded street without incident. I kept my hat pulled low and never met anyone's eyes.

By the time we reached the livery, I figured I'd lost at least fifteen pounds of sweat. Once inside, I tied the sorrel gelding to a snubbing post, and Perkins showed me to a small room in the rear of the livery. He rummaged through a battered rolltop desk and came out with an almost empty quart jar of a clear liquid.

"Reckon you could use a touch. Make it myself."

I grinned. "I reckon." It burned all the way down to the pit of my belly. If I had any germs in my system, they were all dead or dying now.

He gestured to the cot next to the wall. "Sit. Tell me all about what you and Cletus come up with."

Fifteen minutes and two drinks later, I finished my story. "There were four different brands in the herd. Shouldn't be hard to find out if they were stolen or not."

Perkins frowned, the wrinkles on his weathered face running together like furrows in a plowed field. "Who's going to arrest him? He's the law here."

Before I had a chance to answer, a voice called out Perkins's name. I grabbed for my sixgun, but the lanky liveryman held up his hand and shook his head. "Probably some drunk looking for a place to sleep it off. Wait here. I'll be right back."

Still tense, I nodded.

Perkins failed to shut the door completely. Staying on the balls of my feet, I eased to the crack between the edge of the door and the jamb.

The interior of the livery was lit by the glow of a small barn lantern. At the edge of the glow, Perkins had his back to me, his lanky body blocking my view of the newcomer. I relaxed enough to let my hand slide off the butt of my Colt.

I started to pour myself another slug of Perkins's homemade rattlesnake juice, but I froze when Perkins hooked his thumb over his shoulder in my direction.

His visitor leaned to one side. I caught my breath when I spotted the crooked nose. Halliburton!

I shucked my sixgun. What the Sam Hill was going on here?

Perkins pointed down the street. Halliburton nodded and hurried away. After a moment, Perkins headed back to the small room.

Flames of anger burned my cheeks. My finger tightened on the trigger. Whatever he was up to, I didn't have time to waste. And gunplay would waste it even faster.

Holstering my Colt, I sat back down on the cot just as Perkins opened the door. I would have hated to play poker with that hombre. His face was pure innocence when he shrugged and commented. "Yep. Just a drunk." He plopped down in the chair by the table and shoved his battered hat to the back of his head. "Now, back to Meechum."

I yawned and shook my head. "Let it wait some. I need some sleep. Wake me in an hour."

"Why sure," he replied, rising and tugging his hat forward. "And don't worry. You're safe here."

The moment he turned his back to me, I jammed

the muzzle of my Colt in his back. "Not a word, Perkins. Don't even breathe."

"Hey, what—"

He started to turn, so I whopped him upside the head. He dropped like a poleaxed hog.

I turned off the lamp in the small room. Moments later, I extinguished the barn lantern and led the gelding out the back door. I spotted my own calico pony in the corral. He recognized me and whinnied. For a moment, I considered throwing the saddle on him, but if Meechum spotted the sorrel gelding in the corral, he'd know that Jenny Ryan had given me assistance.

Once on the prairie, I turned north, heading for the Circle R. I'd start with Jenny Ryan and go from there.

Just after sunrise, I reined up just below the crest of a sandhill and watched as the buckboard carrying Jenny and the children bounced along the road to Hidetown. I backed the gelding down a step or two so I wouldn't be silhouetted.

I guessed they were heading in for Jackson's funeral. At least Tevis and Old Watts were at the ranch. They could help.

The two old men were eager to help.

I'd turned the gelding loose and stuck my head under the water pump to wash the dust off my head and the sleep from my eyes. "I don't know if you old boys know it or not, but there's a heap of rustling going on in this neck of the woods."

Tevis grunted and squirted an arc of tobacco juice on the ground. "You ain't telling us nothing we don't know, young feller." He gestured toward the cook shack. "Looks like you could put yourself around some grub and hot coffee."

"Sounds mighty good to me," I replied, falling into step with the two old–timers.

Old Watts pushed the tip of his tongue through the narrow gap where his two front teeth had once resided. "I been telling Missy Jenny that Meechum ain't no gooder than a common thief."

I shook my head and dried my face with my neckerchief. "I didn't say nothing about Meechum."

Tevis spoke up. "Didn't need to. Ever'one with good sense knows he's behind all the rustling going on. It's just nobody has been able to prove it."

"Yep," Old Watts replied. "Them that even thinks about it ends up like old Cletus, deader'n a stomped-on cockroach."

I halted. For a moment, I stared at the old men in disbelief. "Then why don't folks do something about it? I know Meechum runs things, but citizens could get together."

Old Watts removed his tattered hat and eyed Tevis with misgiving. "Well, sir, not ever'one believes Meechum is the guilty one." He headed for the cook shack again.

Tevis puffed up. The tip of his ears turned red. He shifted his wad of tobacco to the other cheek and grabbed Old Watts's arm. "You old coot. You calling me a liar?"

I almost bumped into the cantankerous pair.

Jutting out his bearded jaw, Old Watts retorted, "Not a liar, just kinda slow in the head. You know as well as me that half of Hidetown don't want things to change."

"Why, sure I do. But that don't mean they don't know or at least suspect what Meechum has been up to."

Old Watts looked back at me. "That's why we ain't never going to get folks there to throw Meechum out. The stores, the saloons, they're all taking in the greenbacks. They're happy as a fly on a hot apple pie. That's why they won't let theyselves believe he's guilty." He shot a finger in the direction of the cook shack. "Come on. I'm ready for some coffee."

I fell into step with them once again. "I reckon I see your point. It is hard for a jasper to turn away good money, and I suspect it is a natural thing to look the other way when you don't like what you see."

Old Watts kicked at the hardpan with his boot.

"But, we still have the problem of rustling," I said as we entered the shack and slid in at the hand-hewn table. "What about the Circle R? You sold any stock lately, horses or cows?"

Tevis puckered his lips and shook his head. "Nope."

"Why you asking?" Old Watts said, pouring the coffee and setting a tin plate of cold biscuits and curly bacon on the table.

Tevis scooted a jar of molasses in front of me.

"Well, it's like this." I told them about the stolen herd at Fort Reedstrom while I sipped the coffee between bites of molasses-covered biscuits and bacon. "I know enough about the law that if a crime is committed on government property, then the government can go after the guilty parties."

Old Watts squinted at me. "What do that mean?"

Tevis snorted. "And you called me slow in the head. Why, what this young feller means is that the government has got jer—jury dictate—"

I supplied the word Tevis was looking for. "Jurisdiction."

"Yeah. That. Jurisdiction anywhere, even in Hidetown. Ain't that right?" He looked up at me.

"That's right. If we can get proof that Meechum sold stolen animals to the army, then maybe the army will go after him."

The old men scooted forward, expectant grins on their faces. "What do we do?"

I pulled out the brown paper wrapping on which I had drawn the other brands. "You know who owns these?"

Old Watts nodded. "Yep. What about them?"

"These were the brands on the stock the army bought from Meechum. I'll wait here. You go to the ranchers and find out if they're missing any stock. If they are, tell them I know where it is, and if they want to know, then they can meet me tonight."

"Reckon you might as well meet here," Tevis said in a drawl. "Jenny and the kids is spending the night in Hidetown."

I grinned. "Sounds good to me. By the way," I added, "don't tell them my name. I don't want Meechum surprising us tonight."

After they rode out, I found me an out-of-the-way spot in the hayloft and grabbed some shut-eye.

Chapter Nine

George Teague of the Cross T, Frank Noble of the Bar N, and Cass Adams of the BBB sat around the table in the cook shack, the frowns on their sun-darkened faces deepened by the shadows cast by the coal oil lamp as I told them what I had seen at the fort.

Typical of western ranchers, the three were leathery-tough and their eyes blazed with the desire for revenge on the rustlers.

"I've lost close to two hundred head just this last year," Teague said, running his fingers through his thinning white hair. "I ain't sold none neither. If you saw my stock at the fort, then it was stolen."

Adams and Noble chimed in. The latter cleared his throat. "But, I got me a question, Quinlan. I know why you didn't want Old Watts to tell me who you were, but I want to know just what you've got to gain from all this. These ain't your beeves. This won't prove you didn't kill that cowpoke."

"Fair question, Noble. A simple answer. I don't want to have to run from something I didn't do. I've seen enough to tie Meechum and the dead cowpoke into the rustling, but I got no one to back me up. To make matters worse, Cletus Jackson told Bert Perkins everything he had learned. Perkins passed the information to Meechum, and now the sheriff has to get rid of me because I know too much."

The three ranchers exchanged cautious looks.

Old Watts spoke up. "What we got in mind is to ride over to the fort. See if your stock is still there."

"What if it ain't?" Adams frowned.

"They'll have records," I said. "By brand as well as the seller."

"Meechum ain't dumb enough to use his own name."

"Makes no difference. They'll recognize him regardless of the name he's using."

I had no way of knowing, but Jack Meechum had got wind that something was up, and he was making plans to ensure that his profitable little enterprise would suffer no harm.

* * *

During the night, the wind picked up from the southeast. We reached Fort Reedstrom early next morning. When we topped the rise overlooking the fort, a grin leaped to my lips. There was still twenty or so head of beeves and horses in the corrals.

Gusts of wind kicked up the dust and sand, leaving a layer of the gritty substance on every exposed surface. By the time a jasper muttered two words, there was enough sand on his teeth to plant corn.

Frank Noble cursed when he spotted several head of Bar N stock milling about the corral. Teague clenched his teeth when he saw Cross T beeves mixed in. He looked around at me. "You was sure enough telling us the truth, Quinlan."

"Reckon so," Adams put in. He looked around. "Let's us go find the man that runs this place."

Resting his chin on his steepled fingers, Colonel Warren Trout Harris listened carefully as we laid out our story and accusations. Behind him, the American flag was draped across the wall. A sergeant stood at attention beside the closed door.

The colonel pursed his lips when we finished. "Those are quite serious allegations against . . ." He glanced at the paper in his hand. "Against John Morris, gentlemen. The man you call Jack Meechum."

George Teague nodded emphatically. "That's what we're saying. How else do you soldier boys figure my stock got here?"

Colonel Harris continued. "Naturally, the army had no way of knowing they were stolen—if they were, but if you gentleman are willing to file charges, then the army will investigate them since an illegal act was perpetrated on our reservation."

Frank Noble grunted. "We're more than willing, colonel. Let's get on with it."

The others muttered their agreement.

Colonel Harris was an experienced post officer. He knew that his first obligation was to keep the local citizens happy, corral the Indians second, and third, rid the state of as many undesirables as possible.

"I'm sending Lieutenant Wyler and a small detachment of cavalry, gentlemen. Lieutenant Wyler is our procurement officer, and as such, has had several dealings with John Morris, the man you call Meechum. If the two are the same, he will recognize him. If so, he has orders to arrest the man and his gang and return them to the post for a trial."

We rode within the hour, striking out across the prairie toward Hidetown. The wind was steady from the southeast, peppering our exposed flesh with grains of sand, and moaning like a thousand lost souls searching for their coffins. The sky turned a dull red, growing deeper and darker as the sun dropped beneath the horizon.

Lieutenant Wyler opted to camp in the bend of a dry creek bed with high bluff walls, out of the wind. But the moaning of the wind remained constant.

Below the surface of the prairie, we failed to notice when the wind shifted more to the east. Next morning, thickening clouds sped past, and as the morning passed, pockets of light rain began to spray us.

The lieutenant kept us on a direct path toward Hidetown, a strategy that made me a little nervous. But, I figured he must know what he was doing. Still, the hair on the back of my neck bristled. Things seemed to be going too easy.

Mid-morning, the light rain turned heavy. Within minutes, we were all soaked. "Maybe it'll pass over," Cass Adams said, staring hopefully at the dark clouds sweeping rapidly to the west.

"Reckon it will," Noble put in. "I don't hear no thunder or lightning."

I studied the weather. Years before down on the gulf coast, I had run into a couple storms similar to the way this one was developing. "I don't think so. This looks like one of those hurricanes that's blown ashore."

Lieutenant Wyler glanced around at me. "You sure, Mister Quinlan?"

"Nope. Just saying it looks like one. If it is, we can expect several hours of steady rain, some heavy, some light, but steady." I glanced over my shoulder, noting not just the scudding clouds, but the surrounding sandhills, which for some reason now seemed ominous.

We rode hunched over in our saddles, backs to the

driving rain, too concerned about the elements and not vigilant enough of the prairie.

The rain muffled the first shot. It sounded more like a pop than gunfire, but when we saw Lieutenant Wyler tumble sideways out of his saddle, we knew we had ridden blindly into an ambush.

In the next moment, the hills erupted with a roaring of Winchesters. We were caught in the middle, in a shallow valley. Bushwhackers hidden on the crest of every hill surrounding us poured lead plums into our small, confused party.

I saw Cass Adams's hat leap from his head and his white hair turn red as he tumbled backward off his pony.

Instinctively, we returned fire, aiming only in the direction we thought the bushwhackers were hidden.

I jerked off a shot at a silhouette on the crest of a hill. Frightened, my pony reared and lashed out with his front feet. I tugged on the reins in an effort to bring him back under control. He spun in a circle, probably the only reason I didn't catch a slug. A cacophony of whinnying horses, shouting soldiers, and cursing ranchers sounded above the beating of the heavy rain.

Noble and I locked eyes. I could see the fear in his. "Let's ride," I shouted. "Break out of here." I straightened my horse and slammed my spurs into his flanks. Startled, he leaped forward, and in the next few seconds he was stretching out in a full gallop while I leaned over his neck and returned the bushwhackers' fire.

I had no idea who was behind me, but I wasn't taking the time to look around. Our only chance was to break free of the ambush before they gunned us down to the last man.

Digging a heel into the stirrup for balance, I scooted sideways in the saddle and threw a wild shot off to my right.

Suddenly, a figure rose from behind a sagebush in front of me. I drew down on him and squeezed the trigger. The hammer fell on a spent cartridge. He threw his Winchester to his shoulder, but before he could touch off a shot, I ran over him.

All I remember next was a blow to the back of my head that knocked me forward. I grabbed for the horse's flying mane with both hands. After that, there was nothing but darkness.

Chapter Ten

"**J**ace. Jace."

From somewhere beyond the darkness, I heard my name. Then I felt a cool rag on my forehead. I figured I must have somehow managed to reach heaven, for nobody in Hades would have offered me any comfort. That thought must have somehow satisfied me, for I went back to sleep.

Later, muffled words and the rich aroma of honest-to-goodness sixshooter coffee insinuated themselves into my fog-cloaked brain. I cracked one eye open. Light poured in. I moved slightly and felt the confines of a feather mattress supporting me.

I opened both eyes and stared at the puncheoned ceiling over my head.

"Jace. You're awake." Danny Ryan's beaming face

moved into my line of vision. He wore a grin as wide as the Red River. "You're awake."

A feminine voice came from somewhere with a giggle. "You already said that once, silly."

Danny's grin fluttered, then returned. "Hush up, Emmabelle. Go tell Jenny that Jace is awake."

Retreating footsteps told me she was doing as he said. I drew my tongue over my dry lips.

"Thirsty? Here." He held a dipper of cool water to my lips. I leaned up and took a few refreshing sips. It tasted better than any coffee or whiskey I'd ever tossed down my gullet.

Moments later, Jenny returned with Old Watts and Tevis at her heels. Unsmiling, she eyed me a moment, laid her hand on my forehead, and then nodded. "You know where you are?"

I tried to grin. "Looks like the Circle R."

A faint smile ticked up the edge of her lips. "Well, at least your brain isn't addled. You took a powerful blow on the back of your head."

"Yep," Old Watts drawled. "It been any deeper, your brains would have leaked out."

Questions filled my head. "How—how did I get here? Last I remember, I . . ." In the next instant, my eyes closed and I drifted back into that familiar darkness.

"He's asleep," Tevis muttered.

I wasn't asleep. It was strange. I was swimming in all that darkness, but I could hear their every word.

"Then let him," Jenny said. "What he needs now is rest."

With a grunt, Old Watts said, "What do you reckon he'll do when he wakes up?"

Jenny whispered. "With both the sheriff and the army after him, he'd best light a shuck out of Texas."

I tried to open my eyes, but they refused the commands my brain was sending. I wanted to speak, to find out just what she meant, but the words wouldn't come. All I could do was lie there and wonder.

It was late afternoon when I awakened. Danny was staring down at me. He grinned when I moved my head and looked up at him. "How do you feel?"

"About as good as I could expect, I reckon." I blinked once or twice to get the sleep from my eyes.

He offered a dipper of water. "Thirsty?"

I leaned up and drank the whole dipperful, then fell back on my pillow, exhausted from the effort. "How long I been here?"

"Three days. We heard a noise in the barn early one morning. The horse you borrowed was in the barn with the saddle on. As soon as the sun came up, we back-tracked and found you a couple miles out." He shook his head. "You sure was lucky, Jace. All that rain kept the sand hard enough we could follow the horse's tracks. If it had been that old loose sand, we'd never been able to backtrack him."

"I'm right glad you did."

"Good thing we found you when we did. A big old lobo wolf was sniffing around."

"Well, see you decided to join the living." I looked around as Jenny swept into the room, a faint smile on her face, but a glitter in her eyes. "We were beginning to wonder if you were just going to sleep your life away."

"Well . . ." I tried to sit up, but she placed a tiny hand on my shoulder and pressed me back.

"Just stay where you are. Let's get some broth down you. Start building you back up." She nodded to Danny. "Get him some broth and coffee, will you Danny?"

"Sure, Jenny." With a big grin, he hurried from the room.

Jenny grew serious. "You're in a mess of trouble, Jace." She hesitated. Her cheeks colored when she realized she'd called me by my given name. "I mean, Mister Quinlan. I—"

"Please, Miss Jenny. Jace is fine."

She smiled demurely and then grew serious once again. "Sheriff Meechum and the U.S. Army are searching for you. They've put out a dead-or-alive wanted on you." I frowned, but she held up her hand. "Cass Adams, George Teague, Frank Noble, and the entire detachment of cavalry were shot and killed. Meechum claims you did it."

My brain reeled. I had the feeling I was viewing all of this from another plane, from far above, and it was nothing but a stage play. All I could do was stare at her in open-mouthed astonishment. Finally, I managed to croak out, "That isn't true. I—"

She laid her hand on mine. "I know, I know."

"You do?" I studied her a moment, really puzzled now. "How? Why should you think any different? After all, you and the sheriff . . . well, you know."

"Yes," she nodded. "I know, but that has nothing to do with this. Old Watts and Tevis told me about the ranchers and the brands. So, when we found you, I rode over to Fort Reedstrom to see for myself."

I held my breath.

"What I saw and learned convinced me. According to the records Colonel Harris showed me, someone has sold the army over three hundred head of Circle R stock over the past few years."

"Meechum," I interjected.

"That's what Tevis and Old Watts say, but I don't see enough proof of his guilt."

Trying to keep my voice calm and level, I asked, "You said Meechum claims I did it. How does he know?"

"He saw you. He said he and some of his deputies were out searching for rustlers when they heard gunfire. When they reached the spot, he saw you riding away. He said they chased you, but you dodged them. They loaded up the dead then."

I had to hand it to Meechum. He could come up with one slick story after another. The problem with slick stories though is that a jasper has to remember them. "According to him, when did all this happen?"

A tiny frown knit her forehead. She chewed on her lip thoughtfully. "Let's see. This is Friday. Must have been Wednesday. Yes, that's when. Wednesday."

Suddenly, I saw the crack in his story. "When did you all find me?"

She counted back on her fingers. "Wednesday morning." She hesitated, recognizing the point I was trying to make. "I don't know how far you were when we found you, from where the ambush took place. The time could work, although I don't believe you did it."

"You're forgetting one thing, and it should be enough to convince you I'm telling the truth and Meechum is lying."

She arched an eyebrow. "And what might that be?"

At that moment, Danny returned with the coffee and broth. Tevis and Old Watts shuffled in behind him, grinning.

I spoke to the youth. "Danny, when did you find the horse I borrowed? The one out in the barn."

Jenny's eyes grew wide in sudden understanding. She pressed her fingers to her lips and answered the question I had asked of Danny even before the young man could utter a word. "That's right. It was early morning. Before sunrise." I nodded, and she continued. "That means he couldn't have seen you riding away. The horse was here in the barn, and you were lying out on the prairie."

"Exactly. That isn't his first mistake. The first was when they accused me of killing Obery Phillips. Meechum claimed he had met Obery Phillips the day before." I explained to her about the red plaid shirt. "Cletus Jackson caught the mistake too. That's why he believed me, and that's why he was shot. Bert Perkins saw it also, but he's tight with the sheriff. I was lucky to get out of his place when I did."

No one spoke for several moments. We just stared at each other, each lost with his own thoughts and wondering what the future held in store.

Finally, in a small, almost frail voice, she whispered, "We don't have a chance, do we? I mean as long as Jack is sheriff."

Old Watts snorted. "I ain't afraid of Meechum, Miss Jenny. We're here with you."

She gave him a weak smile.

I raised up on one elbow. "One thing is certain, we can't ask the army for help, and another thing is that you can't let the sheriff even suspect what you know." I looked each one in the eye. "None of you."

She shook her head slowly, the pain she felt evident in the wrinkles in her forehead and the hurt in her eyes. "He was always nice to us, a friend. I know he wanted more, but . . ." She shrugged. "I've learned this is a hard land. A person has to be practical. Sometimes that special feeling between two people isn't there, but you have to go on. You have to make do. I understand that, and I don't fault anyone for it." She shook her head. "But now to learn he was stealing Circle R stock all the while he was courting me . . . I don't know if I could forgive that."

I didn't know what to say to soothe her pain. I was awkward with words, especially around women. I started to keep quiet, figuring that was better than causing her more pain, but I had to say something. "I'm sorry, Miss Jenny."

She stared at me dully. "Thank you, Mister Quinlan."

Tevis cleared his throat. "What do you reckon on doing now, Jace?"

Jenny spoke up. "He's got no choice. He's got to leave the country soon as he's fit to ride."

That's the moment I knew what I had to do.

I looked at Danny. "Get my duds for me." I sat up and swung my legs off the side of the bed. A wave of dizziness washed over me, but I grabbed the mattress with both hands to steady me until the spell passed. The back of my head pounded. With my eyes squeezed shut, I muttered. "I been here three days. I got to ride. We're all lucky Meechum hasn't thought to come up here."

Jenny protested.

"He's right," Old Watts said. "If Meechum figures we know what's going on, he'll take care of us like he has all the others."

"I just can't believe he'd do anything like that to us," Jenny replied, shaking her head.

Danny returned with my clothes. I looked around at Jenny, but the pounding in my head blurred my vision. "You—you best step out. I got to—to—"

I closed my eyes tight and held to the mattress. Sweat popped out of every pore in my skin, drenching my long johns.

Tevis spoke up. "Maybe Jenny's right. Maybe you best rest a mite longer."

I opened my eyes and focused them on a wooden peg in the far wall. "No. The spell's passing. I'll make it. Just get me a sound horse and a proper warbag."

"Where you plan on heading first?"

"Somewhere on the Canadian. It'll be dark soon. I don't think I could take that hot sun, not with my head feeling like a green bronc kicked it. I'll find me a spot to hole up for a few days. Then I'll come back." I blinked several times, trying to focus on the gap-toothed grin of Old Watts. "I promise you, I'll be back. Just take care of Jenny and the kids."

Tevis grunted. "Don't you worry none, son. You'll have a warbag and the best animal we got."

Old Watts chuckled. "You bet."

Jenny met me outside in an effort once again to persuade me to remain a few more days. "But your head—that's a bad injury."

"I been hurt before, and I'll be hurt again, but I'll get through them."

She stood in the middle of Danny and Emmabelle.

Tevis and Old Watts stood behind them. "Take care," she replied, forcing a weak smile.

The sun dropped below the horizon, and with the gray of dusk, the air cooled, its soothing touch on my cheeks giving me renewed energy.

I had a handful of dizzy spells that night, but I held tightly to the saddle horn and rode them down. The throbbing in my head had dulled by the time I reached the Canadian River just before sunup. Unfamiliar with the river, I pulled into a small grove of hackberry and willow until there was enough light for me to find a proper hidey-hole for the next few days.

I tied my horse to a hackberry and loosened the cinch to give him some breathing room. The bubbling and swishing of the river as it swept past were an irresistible lure to its cool waters. I plunged my head and shoulders into the cold water and shook like a dog, enjoying the tingle the chilly water gave my skin. Then I drank deeply, after which I returned to my small grove to await the sun.

I studied the horse the Circle R had given me. From the night's ride, I knew the animal had staying power. He was strong, had a naturally fast-paced gait, and as I looked over his conformation, I saw why. Deep-chested and long-legged, the sorrel had attentive eyes and a clean, well-shaped head.

"You must be the pick of the litter, boy," I whispered, patting him on the neck and running my hands down his shoulders and legs.

The saddlebags bulged with grub, and cartridges for the .44 on my hip and the Winchester in the boot. A faint smile played over my lips. When Tevis packed a warbag, he packed a warbag.

With the rising of the sun, I moved out, my gaze constantly sweeping the horizon a few deliberate degrees at a time. Within an hour, I found an ideal camp in the middle of a thick cluster of cottonwood on the crest of a bluff with a 360-degree field of view.

The tall trees and their thick canopy of leaves winnowed my campfire smoke into indiscernible wisps by the time it drifted beyond the crown of fluttering leaves.

I sat the coffeepot in the coals at the edge of the fire. A surge of dizziness hit. I closed my eyes and grabbed at the trunk of a nearby cottonwood. As the lightheadedness passed, I heard the rushing of the river.

The sudden urge to soak my weary bones in the icy water came over me. Without another thought, I quickly undressed down to my long johns and, sixgun in hand, waded into the river. I shivered at the bracing chill of the water.

I lay prone, my head on a water-soaked log, and let the water rush over me. The throbbing slowly dissipated.

Wading ashore, I hung my long johns on a limb to dry, and there, bare as the day I was born, poured a cup of coffee and put some bacon on to fry.

Chapter Eleven

After a hot breakfast, I slipped into my dry clothes and rolled out my soogan. I slept in snatches the rest of the day, awakening at each sound.

The next day as I lazed about the camp, I began making my plans. I was facing six men, all gunnies, all owlhoots with nothing to lose. The only one of the six for whom I had any concern was young Bud Tunney. He was there because Meechum was family. The other four deputies—Carstairs, Halliburton, Burgess, and Gotrain—meant nothing to me. They were human trash like the two scavengers who murdered my pa back in '61.

I've heard people say if you cut off the head of the snake, the body will die. I reckon that'll work if a jasper can manage it, but I couldn't figure any way to get to Meechum without facing the other five.

On the other hand, if you get rid of a centipede's legs, all he can do is wallow about on the ground.

I reached for the coffeepot. As a stream of thick, sixshooter coffee filled the tin cup, I knew what I had to do. Meechum was my centipede, and I had to cut off his legs.

Of course, I reminded myself, a jasper starts fooling around with centipedes, he's liable to get bit himself.

What I had to figure out was how to get rid of the deputies. Naturally, if they just up and decided to leave the country, all of us would find it less stressful.

Maybe there was someway I could encourage them to make such a decision. On the other hand, I realized that some might not take too kindly to my encourage-ment.

That being the situation, I might have to resort to more direct methods. Absently, I slipped my .44 up and down in the holster, reassuring myself by the slick feel as it slid in and out.

I fashioned three bags from my blankets and spent the rest of the day looking for snakes. I found my last one that night, a fat and sassy rattlesnake, the maestro of my snake sonata.

The glow of the campfire drew him into camp. I dropped him into a bag of his own after tying a length of rawhide around his rattles. I secured the neck of his sack, then dropped it into a second bag, taking care to leave the rawhide protruding when I tied the neck of the sack.

I then rolled the two sacks up and fit the whole shebang into one pocket of the saddlebags. The third bag, I tied to the back of the cantle. I had managed to snare a dozen or so water snakes and grass snakes. Non-poisonous, but just as frightening. I slid a branch with a Y-fork in the pouch with my Winchester.

Well before sunrise, I camped on a sandhill a couple miles east of Hidetown. After dark, I'd ride in closer, and then move on in by foot.

I spent the day readying my gear and watching the town.

Wagons rolled in and out of the small village.

Throughout the blistering day, I kept my pets in the shade, occasionally dampening the bags with water from my canteen.

As the sun dropped beneath the western horizon in a stunning display of purple and gold, I swung into the saddle and rode closer to Hidetown. Half-a-mile outside, I reined up and tied my pony to an oak in a small patch of shinnery.

With a bag in each hand and the Y-forked branch under my belt, I headed for Hidetown which, as usual, roared with laughter, curses, gunshots, and singing women. I deposited the bags beneath a sagebush near the sheriff's outhouse. I caught my breath and wrinkled my nose. It was sure ripe.

I searched the darkness between me and the sheriff's office. Beyond the office, the street rocked with noise, but the alley was silent as a funeral home.

Remaining in a crouch, I ghosted to the jail and peered over the windowsill. I jerked my head down and pressed into the shadows next to the wall. The fat deputy, Gotrain, was straddling a stool at the table, shoveling beans down his gullet. His hat was on the table, and his bald head glistened in the yellow lamplight.

I hazarded a second glance, quickly taking in the remainder of the dimly-lit jail. I grimaced. A cowpoke lay on the cot, his back to me. Muttering a curse, I hurried back to the sagebush beneath which I had hidden my little pets. I still had the first part of my plan.

When I reached the outhouse, I dropped one bag on the ground. I had to work fast. I glanced at the jail. Light poured out the side window and spilled onto the ground.

Opening the outhouse door, I grabbed the length of rawhide protruding from the first sack. I slipped one end over a rafter, pulled both bags a couple feet off the floor and fastened the other end of the rawhide to a bent nail in the door.

The bags remained ominously motionless. I tested my plan once or twice by opening and closing the door. When I closed the door, the bags touched the floor. When the door opened, the bags rose to about chest high. I grinned, then shot a hasty look at the jail. I opened the outer bag and let it drop.

Now the second bag dangled from the rawhide. Abruptly, it squirmed violently. I froze until the bag ceased jerking about and grew motionless.

I pulled the forked branch from my belt and fit it around the snake inside the bag while I loosened the neck of the sack.

Quickly I stepped back and removed the branch. The bag slid off a fat, angry five-foot rattlesnake dangling by his tail from the rafters of the outhouse. I closed the door, listening to his squirming when his belly touched the floor.

The rattler could go nowhere. He'd slither so far and the rawhide would stop him. Soon, he would be one frustrated, angry rattlesnake.

Sweat stung my eyes. I grabbed the other bag and slipped into the shadows by the jail. I peered inside. Gotrain sat at the table drinking from a bottle of Old Crow. The jasper on the cot had disappeared.

Maybe everything would fall into place. Now, all I had to do was wait.

Time dragged.

The bag at my feet squirmed. I couldn't resist a grim smile. Come morning, maybe there would be one less leg on the centipede.

Inside, Gotrain pushed to his feet. He rubbed his

large belly and headed for the front door. For a moment, I was disappointed, but then I realized this could be my opportunity to set everything in place and then put some distance between me and Hidetown before all the excitement began.

No sooner had he closed the front door than I slipped in the back. I stopped in the middle of the room and looked around for a place to hide the snakes. Footsteps outside the door froze me. I dived under the cot, pulling the bag of snakes with me and tugging the blanket over the edge of the bed to hide me.

Gotrain lumbered back in, paused, belched loudly, then cursed. "Musta been them blasted beans," he muttered. "Tear a jasper to pieces." He grabbed the lantern and headed out the back door, leaving me in the dark except for the moonlight shining through the windows.

As soon as the back door slammed shut, I jumped up on the cot and wedged the bag of snakes between the rafter and the roof joist. I yanked out my knife and sliced the bag.

Five seconds later, I was hurrying down the street when the bloodcurdling scream echoed through the shabby village. I darted between two hide-covered buildings. Before I reached the rear of the buildings, four shots that sounded like one tore the night apart. There was another terrified scream and the sound of wood snapping and shattering.

I disappeared into the prairie. When I glanced over my shoulder, I caught a glimpse of fire.

Moments later, another flurry of gunfire broke the silence of the night.

The next morning, I rode out to the Circle R. Danny ran to meet me. While I was assuring him I was just fine, Jenny and Emmabelle hurried out. Old Watts shuffled out of the barn. He wore a bruise on his left cheekbone.

"I'll tell you over coffee," Jenny said when I asked the old man about the bruise. "Have you had breakfast?"

I shook my head and dismounted, giving Danny the reins. "Take care of him, will you son? Feed him good. He hadn't much to graze on since the Canadian." I glanced around. "Where's Tevis?"

"Rode into Hidetown yesterday to mail a letter. Ought to be back this morning."

It seemed as if I had been away from the Circle R for months, but only a few days had passed. Jenny poured Old Watts and me coffee and busied herself frying bacon and stirring up some red-eye gravy. "It's good you left when you did. Jack showed up early next morning. We denied everything, but he was suspicious."

"He the one that gave you that?" I gestured with my coffee mug at the bruise on Old Watts's face.

"I couldn't believe Jack was so violent. I'd never seen him like that." She shook her head and smiled faintly at Emmabelle. "It's lucky for me I found out just how he can be."

The pounding of hoofbeats interrupted us.

Shucking my sixgun, I peered out the window in time to see Tevis rein his pony up to the hitching rail. He whipped the reins around the rail and half-limped, half-ran to the house.

"Tevis! What on earth!" Jenny exclaimed when the old man slid to a halt next to the table.

A broad grin split his thin face. "You all ain't going to believe it. You just ain't going to believe it at all." He chuckled and shook his head. "It was sure something to see."

Old Watts growled. "Well, stop cackling like an old hen and let us in on the big secret."

His eyes danced with amusement. "It couldn't happened to a more deserving jasper, either. It—"

Jenny interrupted. "Tevis!"

"Huh?" He looked around at her, puzzled.

She placed her fork in her plate and smiled. "What happened?"

He shook his head. "Gotrain. The deputy?"

That got my attention. I paused with a chunk of bacon poised on the tines of my fork. "What about him?"

"Well, sir, best we could figure, he went to the outhouse last night. There was a rattlesnake in there. He shot at it and jumped to the side." He started chuckling again. "Sorry, but when I think about it . . ."

"Blast it, old man. What happened?" Old Watts barked.

His eyes dancing, Tevis continued. "When old fat Gotrain jumped, the outhouse caved in."

Jenny gasped. Danny laughed.

"There it went—outhouse, rattler, coal oil lantern, and old Gotrain down into the pit. By the time we got there, the rattler was trying to climb up one side and Gotrain up the other. And the fire was burning in the middle. Some jasper spotted the rattler and shot it." He paused. "Funny thing," he added, looking at me, "there was a length of rawhide tied to the snake's rattles. Like someone had deliberately strung it up in the outhouse."

I took a bite of bacon. "Now who would do something like that?"

Impatiently, Old Watts said, "Well, then what happened? Gotrain get out?"

"Not until two old buffalo skinners who stunk worse'n Gotrain drug him out." He held his nose with one hand and waved the other in front of it. "Lordy. He stunk like a dead polecat."

We all laughed. "He sure deserved it," Old Watts remarked.

"That ain't all." Tevis shook his head emphatically. "No, sir. Them skinners helped him to the jail and plopped him down on the cot. Gotrain, he was jabbering away like one of them church folks that bite the head off chickens. Anyways, they laid him down on the cot, and I'll be horn-swoggled if a whole basketful of snakes didn't fall from the ceiling right down on top of him."

Jenny gasped and pressed her fingers to her lips. "What then?"

The grin on Tevis' face faded. "When them snakes hit him, his legs and arms shot up in the air like a spider." He hesitated, his wrinkled face growing somber. "He give out a terrible scream and then dropped dead."

I clenched my teeth and closed my eyes.

"Old Doc Spencer says Gotrain's heart just gave out. He was fat and always huffing and puffing wherever he went. According to the doc, Gotrain's heart could've gone out just walking down the street."

He glanced at me. I thought I saw a knowing grin on his face, but when I looked again, it had vanished.

Jenny looked around. "Were you in Hidetown last night, Jace?"

Five sets of eyes turned on me. Casually, I sipped my coffee. "Let me put it this way, Miss Jenny. You're all better off if you don't know anything about me. That way, you can't be accused of nothing."

Before she could reply, I rose from the table. "Saying that, I best be riding on. I wouldn't at all be surprised if the sheriff doesn't pay you a visit."

Jenny didn't argue. She couldn't. She knew I was right.

Twenty minutes after I rode out, I spotted a cloud of dust south of the ranch, coming directly from Hidetown.

Chapter Twelve

I headed back to the Canadian where I could decide on my next move.

One down. Five to go. Four if I didn't count young Bud Tunney. On the other hand, he might decide to throw in whole hog with his uncle.

My emotions were mixed concerning Gotrain. I told myself I had simply wanted to scare him off, yet deep down I had known that he wouldn't run, or that even if he wanted to hightail out of Hidetown, Meechum wouldn't let him.

I had to reconcile myself to the chilling truth that in all likelihood, the remaining deputies would not scare, and that if I got to Meechum, it would have to be over their dead bodies. I laid my hand on the butt of my sidearm. Sooner or later, the Colt would be a part of settling our problem.

Taking no chances, I laid me a small fire early and let it burn down to coals before I fried bacon and boiled coffee. I pulled out a couple of cold biscuits Jenny had packed. I sliced them in two and dropped them in the bacon grease. When they were soaked with hot grease, I folded the bacon between them.

Hot coffee and bacon sandwiches. I licked my lips.

I doubt if the Palmer House in Chicago served such fare in its dining room, but on the banks of the Canadian River that night, it was a right proper feast.

Dusk moved in, and before I could finish my coffee, the stars started popping out of a sky that was black as a crow's wing.

My sorrel grazed contentedly. Suddenly, he lifted his head and perked his ears forward. I stepped away from the coals even though they put off little light. From downriver came the splashing of a single pony crossing the river in the shallows.

I shucked my sixgun and stepped into the shadows of a cottonwood.

A dark figure appeared out of the night, silhouetted against the silvery water. The figure's stature was slight, like a woman or a young boy.

The horse and rider drew closer. The starlight reflected off his face. I frowned. Danny? I waited. The rider drew near.

"Hold it," I said softly, my voice carrying above the bubbling of the river.

The rider yelped in surprise and jerked on the reins. His horse reared, then splashed back into the shallow water. "Who's out there?"

I couldn't believe my ears. "Danny? Danny, is that you?"

"Jace? Jace! Oh, golly. I didn't think I'd ever find you," he said, relief obvious in his voice.

I holstered my handgun and sloshed into the river. Taking the reins, I led horse and rider to my camp.

"What the blazes you doing out here?" I growled as he dismounted.

"Oh, Jace, Jace." He broke into sobs and threw his arms around my waist. I froze, confused. "What's going on?"

He looked up at me and sputtered. "The sheriff. He got there just after you left. He was crazy, yelling and stomping. Busting up furniture when he couldn't find you." He snuffled. "Beat Tevis up bad, and shot Old Watts dead."

His words stunned me. "What?"

"I saw him. I was there. Killed Old Watts dead."

Instinctively, I put my arms around the boy and hugged him to me. "What about Jenny and Emmabelle?"

"Sheriff took them off. When he shot Old Watts, Jenny shoved me out the back door and told me to find you. I watched from a sandhill when they took Jenny and Emmabelle off."

For several minutes, we stood motionless, Danny sobbing into my chest, me with my arms around the boy's quivering shoulders.

I could feel the rage building, heating my blood, throbbing in my ears. Blazing anger consumed any remorse I had felt about Gotrain's fate and a similar fate for the others. At that moment, I could have shot them down with no more regard than I would have for a rabid dog.

Danny slept fitfully that night. I remained awake, listening to the coyotes and wolves, and trying to decide my next step. First was Tevis. After that, I wasn't sure. I poured another cup of coffee and sipped at it as I stared at the young boy slumbering across the fire from me. Whatever I did, I now had another distraction.

Next morning, we rode out early, heading for the Circle R.

A vague plan had taken shape in the back of my brain, one that had taken on a life of its own by the time we pulled up north of the ranch late that afternoon.

Tying the ponies to a sagebush, we eased up the hill and dropped to our bellies, peering through the sage at the ranch house half-a-mile distant. Other than a few horses milling about in the corrals, there was no movement.

I cautioned Danny. "You remember what I said. After dark I'll go in on foot. You stay here with the Winchester. If anything happens to me . . ." I hesitated and shrugged. "Well, son, you take my pony and gear and light a shuck back north. Hidetown and hereabouts won't be none too healthy for you. You hear?"

Danny looked up at me with wide eyes. He swallowed hard. "How—how will I know?"

With a grim chuckle, I said, "Don't worry. You'll know. If nothing happens, I'll wave you in. Just keep your eyes open and that Winchester handy."

"Yes, sir."

Just before sundown, movement at the ranch caught my attention. I squinted into the encroaching dusk. A slight figure limped from the house. Tevis! He slowly made his way to the barn. Moments later he reappeared with a shovel in his hand.

Not far from the back of the house, he began digging.

A sob caught in Danny's throat as the young man did his best not to cry.

The evening grew darker. Soon, Tevis lit a lantern, and in the lonesome glow of a small light there in the middle of the prairie, he dutifully dug a grave for his old friend.

I waited for a light to appear in one of the windows of the main house. I figured if Meechum had left anyone behind, as dark as it was they would have fired up one of the coal oil lanterns.

Laying my hand on Danny's arm, I whispered. "Keep a sharp watch, you hear?"

"Y-y-yes."

I shucked my Colt, and in a crouch, darted from sage to sage, zig-zagging across the prairie toward the ranch house. Once, I spooked up a rabbit that zipped through my legs, scaring me out of a couple years' growth. I dropped to one knee while my heart slowed back down.

Tevis plodded along, one shovelful at a time.

I crept closer, my eyes shifting back and forth between the barn and the house. When I was less than twenty feet from the old man, I ducked behind a sagebush and called out in a whisper. "Tevis!"

He kept digging.

"Tevis," I whispered, louder. "Tevis!"

"Huh!" He jerked his head up and peered into the darkness beyond the glow of the lantern. "Somebody out there?"

"It's me, Jace Quinlan. Don't stop. Keep digging."

He dropped the shovel and climbed out of the grave. "What are you doing out there?" He started toward me.

"No. Keep digging."

The old man paused. The dim glow of the lantern reflected his puzzlement. "What? I don't understand."

If anyone were watching, by now they'd know

something was going on. I blurted out, "You here by yourself?"

Tevis stared at me, then glanced over his shoulder. "You're here."

I remained crouched behind the sage. "I mean, is any of Meechum's men here."

"Oh." He shook his head. "No. They all rode off yesterday. What are you doing back here?"

Still wary, I eyed the dark shadows around the house and barn. "Danny told me what happened."

"Danny!" He looked around. "He's here? He ain't hurt or nothing?"

"He's fine. You sure you're all alone?"

He looked back at the partially completed grave. "Just me and Old Watts. Poor old man. I shoulda planted him yesterday, but I couldn't stand on the gimpy leg." He turned back to me. The pale yellow glow of the lantern glittered on a tear rolling down his leathery cheek. "I never thought I'd see such a day. Not in my life."

I rose and holstered my Colt. "I'll call Danny in and then I'll finish the digging. You rest easy." I stepped into the glow of the lantern and waved to Danny. Moments later, he rode in.

Danny and Tevis laid Old Watts out while I finished the grave. It was midnight when we lowered him. I stepped back and removed my hat. "Anyone got any words to say?"

Danny whispered. "I'll sure miss Old Watts. He

gave me my first chaw of tobacco. I sure got sick. He just laughed. Jenny got mad at him."

Tevis coughed and sniffed. He dug a balled fist in his eye. "Him and me partnered for a long spell. I'll right certain miss him. I'm just an ignorant old man who don't know no good words. Maybe you can say some, Jace."

Both looked at me expectantly. I remembered bits and pieces of the 23rd Psalm. I stared down into the dark hole and whispered, "Yea, though I walk through the valley of the shadow of death, I will fear no evil for Thou art with me. Thy rod and Thy staff, they, ah, they make me feel good. Thou preparest—"

The next few sentences were probably out of order and twisted around, but the idea was there. And even though I probably messed the Psalm up so much that a preacher would cry, and the Ladies Bible Study would probably change churches, we all felt better.

"Amen."

I slapped my hat back on my head and reached for the shovel.

"No," Tevis said, taking the shovel from my hand. "He was my partner. I reckon the last thing I can do for Old Watts is to put the dirt on him."

Chapter Thirteen

Tevis was a tough old bird. Of course, any Texan who managed to survive to his seventies had to be, considering the rigors of the West. Broken bones, gunshot holes, and backside boils were tended at home. Most cowpokes only saw a doctor once a year, and that was usually at the Christmas shindig at the local saloon.

We sat in the dark ranch house peering out the windows. Tevis had boiled some coffee, and we chewed on some hardtack. He insisted in being a part of whatever plan I had. I started to refuse, but I realized that Meechum wouldn't hesitate to kill both Tevis and Danny. Eradicate all witnesses. Why the sheriff didn't kill Tevis when he had the chance, I couldn't guess.

Even though the two would slow me, I felt better having them around.

"We'll use the ranch as a headquarters, but at the first sign of visitors, get out. We'll be better off camping away from the ranch and come in only when necessary."

Danny nodded eagerly, and Tevis grinned. "What's first?"

"First, we have to find out where they took Jenny and Emmabelle."

"How do we do that?" Danny asked.

I poured another cup of coffee and grinned at the two shadows before me. "Here's what I have in mind."

Hackberry and cottonwood interspersed with thorny plum patches grew up and down the sandy banks of Sweetwater Creek. On one side of the creek, a narrow but worn road paralleled the pristine stream. On the other, a narrow horse trail wound its way through the plum patches and cottonwood.

A mile outside of Hidetown, I found the perfect spot for my plan—a small clearing surrounded by cottonwood. Quickly, we built the trap.

"You think that'll work?" Danny eyed the trip log skeptically.

"It'll work," I replied, studying the heavy log leaning against the trunk of a cottonwood.

"I hope so."

I shook my head. "If it doesn't, then I'll keep riding.

He'll stay after me, and you two can head back to the ranch." I swung into the saddle. "Let's us start the stampede."

Tevis and Danny moved north a hundred yards or so, close enough to watch, yet far enough to make their escape if our plan failed.

We had changed ponies back at the Circle R. I rode a short, coupled coyote dun, about as nondescript as an animal could be, the kind no one gave any attention. I crossed the stream where it made a sharp bend and headed down the road to Hidetown.

A quarter-of-a-mile out of town, the stench of the small village hit me. I wrinkled my nose and wondered which of the deputies was watching the town. I figured at least one had to be with Jenny and Emmabelle. That left three, four counting Meechum.

Hidetown was its usual clamorous self with a street jammed with three or four wagons heaped with hides, one or two Conestogas, Morgans, and sixteen-foot freight wagons. Hombres dressed in everything from frock coats to greasy buckskins bustled about the street.

An empty loop hung from the gallows.

I pulled up at the hitching rail of the Buffalo Hide Saloon, the last building before the prairie, and surveyed the town, looking for a familiar face.

I didn't have long to wait. Minutes later, lantern-jawed Joe Carstairs emerged from the sheriff's office.

I grimaced when I saw that red-headed Frank Burgess was right on his heels. Two of them!

We spotted each other at the same time.

I wheeled my dun about and slammed my heels into her flanks. She leaped forward. Within half-a-dozen strides, she was in a full gallop, reaching out and pulling ground past us. The sage blurred as we raced down the road. I glanced over my shoulder. Carstairs was a hundred yards or so back, Burgess another fifteen or twenty.

Ahead, I spotted the bend in the creek. I angled toward the stream. Behind, they were gaining. I grinned as we splashed across the creek and headed down the narrow horse trail. "Just don't stumble," I muttered to the dun. I heard splashing behind me. My grin grew broader. Maybe we would get lucky.

I slowed to draw them in closer.

I slipped my boot from the stirrup as I approached the clearing. Beyond, I spotted the trip log leaning against the cottonwood.

Tightening the reins, I guided the coyote dun between two large cottonwoods. The next second, I kicked the trip log. When it fell, it jerked a hemp rope off the ground and stretched it tautly between two forks in the trees at a height of about six or seven feet.

Reining up, I wheeled the dun about just in time to see Carstairs hit the rope. He started to scream, but the taut rope caught him in the throat, crushing his windpipe. Behind him, Burgess veered to one side and raced between two trees.

The deputy never noticed the ropes we had strung knee-high between each of the trees surrounding the clearing. The first inkling he had that something was amiss was when his pony squealed and dropped out from under him.

Burgess flew through the air, slamming down in the middle of a thorny plum patch. He crashed through the small trees, breaking a leg and shredding his clothes on the thorns. His pony thrashed about several seconds before clambering to his feet and galloping away in fright.

Danny and Tevis hurried in.

I knelt by Carstairs. His head was bent at an odd angle. I knew he was dead, but I checked his heart anyway.

"I saw it," Danny gushed, excited by the events of the last few minutes. "Boy, he hit the rope hard. Why, he spun up on that rope until he was almost standing on his head, and then he fell headfirst to the ground."

I shook my head. "He's dead."

The animated grin faded from Danny's face. "Dead?"

"This one's still alive." Tevis called to us from the plum patch. "Cut up something fierce, but he's alive."

We dragged Burgess from the patch and leaned him up against a cottonwood. The deputy screamed in pain. "My leg. It's busted up bad." Sweat rolled down his face. Pain glazed his eyes. "You got to get me some help."

Tevis snorted. "The kind of help you gave Old Watts?"

The deputy blubbered. "It wasn't me. It was Meechum." He clenched his teeth and moaned. "The pain—I can't stand the pain. Please. Do something." He squeezed his eyes shut.

I squatted by his side. "Where did Meechum take Jenny and Emmabelle Ryan?"

His eyes still closed, he shook his head. "I don't know. He didn't say."

Shucking my sixgun, I touched the muzzle to his broken leg. His eyes popped open, wide with fear.

"Tell you what, deputy," I drawled. "You can stick with that story and stay right here. I'll tie you up good and proper, poke a gag in your mouth, and stick you back in the plum patch. Oh, you'll get the gag out sooner or later, and you'll yell, but I got a feeling no one will hear for awhile." I glanced at his twisted leg. "By that time, gangrene will have taken over that leg. It'll rot off and take you with it. Unless the wolves don't get you first. They can sense when someone is helpless."

Burgess caught his breath.

I stared him straight in the eye. "On the other hand, you tell me what I want to know, I'll straighten the leg, stick you on your horse, and send you back to town." I paused, then added. "One thing. When that leg is healed up all good and proper, you leave Hidetown. Never come back. I ever see you again, I'll shoot you down without even stopping to think about it." Taking a deep breath, I rose and stared down at him.

He remained silent. I shrugged and loosened one of the ropes between the trees.

Tevis spoke up. "You know what you should do, Jace? You ought to loop that rope about his busted leg and tie the other end to his horse. Send them racing across the prairie."

A crazed look filled Burgess's eyes. "You wouldn't let that crazy old man do that, would you?"

I shook out a small loop and dangled it near his foot. I studied him thoughtfully. I looked at Tevis. "You know, that idea never came to me, but now that I consider it, I'll bet that will sure make this old boy's tongue starts wagging. What do you think?"

A wicked grin split Tevis's wrinkled face. "I suspect by the time he's gone fifty yards, he'll sure be a-yelling at the top of his lungs. The only problem," he added, frowning at me, "is that once that horse gets the bit in his teeth, it'll be hard to catch him. We might have to chase him more'n a mile before we could stop him."

I pursed my lips and glanced at Burgess. His face was white as cow's milk. He was trying to form words with his lips but no sound came out. "I don't know if that old leg would even hang together for a mile. Likely as not, after a piece, it'll just pull in two."

Tevis shook his head. "Naw, I don't think so. I figure it'll hang together until we can stop the horse."

"You're wrong about that. I'll bet you five dollars it'll bust apart."

Shaking his head and chuckling, Tevis kept our game going. "Put up your money. This'll be the easiest five dollars I ever made. Why—"

"Hold it up," Burgess screeched. "You can't do that to another person. It ain't human. It ain't."

"Well, now, deputy," I said. "I just like to know who's going to stop us? You sure ain't." With a sudden flick of my wrist, I whipped the loop about his ankle and yanked it tight and gave his busted leg a jerk. "Danny, bring his horse over here."

Burgess screamed in pain and grabbed his leg. He began squealing. "All right, all right. No more, no more. Please. Meechum's got them out north, at the canyon."

"Where you keep the stolen horses and cattle you sell to the army?"

He nodded emphatically. "Yes, yes. At the cabin on the side of the east wall."

"Who's with them?"

"Bud Tunney. Halliburton's supposed to go out today and relieve Bud." He grimaced and held his leg. "Please. Do something. I can't stand the pain."

"Can't do nothing for the pain."

He gasped. "I got almost a full bottle of whiskey in the saddlebags."

I nodded to Danny. He ran to the horse. "I can set the leg for you. It'll heal proper, but you won't never be the same. You'll have a gimpy leg that'll pain you something fierce if you do much riding."

Danny handed me the bottle, and I passed it on to Burgess who greedily downed several large gulps— too fast because he choked and spat up half of what he had drunk.

I knelt by his foot and gripped his ankle. "All right. Best you lean back and grit your teeth. This will be a powerful hurt, but when I finish, the bones will be in place."

Sweat dripped from his jowls. His shirt clung to his chest. He took another quick drink and nodded.

Without hesitation, I yanked hard. He screamed and jerked forward, then fainted, falling back against the cottonwood. Quickly, I set the bones, splinted the leg with dry branches, and wrapped it up with a length of hemp rope.

Behind me, Danny mumbled. "Boy, that looked like it sure hurt."

"It did, boy," Tevis said. The old man spoke to me. "You really going to turn him loose? He'll head straight back to Hidetown and Meechum."

"It's likely."

"We can't let him do that, Jace," Danny said.

They were both right. Depending on how fast Burgess got back to Hidetown, Meechum could be right on our tail by the time we reached the canyon. "How do we stop him?" I gestured to the unconscious deputy. "You want to shoot him right here?"

Danny shook his head. "I don't want to shoot nobody, but he probably will tell what happened, won't he?"

"He could. If he goes back."

Tevis frowned at me. "If he goes back? What's to keep him from going back?"

I began gathering the ropes. "Danny, build us a small fire. Coffee and bacon sounds good. We'll wait until our guest wakes up and have a final talk with him. Maybe we can persuade him that it would be poor judgment on his part if he went back to Hidetown."

"How do you reckon to do that?" Tevis' frown deepened.

"Well, I got a thought on that. It might not work, but I don't have the stomach to kill some jasper in cold blood."

Chapter Fourteen

Burgess awakened while we were cleaning up our utensils and dousing the fire. Immediately, he took another long drink. His eyes were glazed from whiskey and pain. He stared blankly at his leg.

"It's as good a job as most sawbones," I said. "Keep off it best you can."

Burgess nodded silently.

I knelt in front of him and pulled out my knife. Absently, I ran my thumb up and down the blade.

"Now deputy, I want to make a suggestion as to how you can live to a ripe old age. We're going to help you on your horse, give you some water and grub, and point you for Atascosa. Now, I won't lie and tell you it'll be easy getting there, not in your shape. It'll take about four, maybe five days. You take it nice and easy, rest along the way, and you should make it with no problems.

"On the other hand, if you go back to Hidetown, you'll have to tell Meechum what happened. He'll make you, and you know it. You do that, you tell him, then one day or one night, you'll have an unexpected visitor just like Gotrain."

His eyes grew wide, and he stared at me in disbelief. "You—you did that?"

In a blur, I touched the tip of my blade to the point of his Adam's apple. "You won't get away from me. You go back to Hidetown, and I'll guarantee you won't live a week." Just as suddenly, I pulled the blade away, sheathed the knife, and rose to my feet. "Okay, boys. Let's put the deputy on his horse."

When he was mounted, I handed him the reins and stepped back. "Hidetown's behind you. Atascosa is straight ahead."

He hesitated, then clicked his tongue, and rode straight ahead.

Danny stood at my side. "You think he'll go to Atascosa, Jace?"

I studied the retreating back of the deputy. "I don't know, son. That jasper, he isn't too bright. I just don't know what he will do."

Before heading north for the Circle R and then the canyon, we scooped out a shallow grave for Carstairs and took his horse with us. Meechum would be puzzled. Sooner or later, he'd figure out something, but at least we'd have some time to play with.

At the Circle R, we restocked out grub, changed ponies, and rode out. We'd camp north of the ranch.

We crossed the Canadian River next morning. Having traveled the country a week or so earlier with Cletus Jackson, I managed to keep my bearings fairly well. I pointed northeast. "The canyon is in that direction."

"How far?" Tevis asked.

"Sundown, but we'll swing wide, come in from behind. Whoever is watching the girls will probably keep his eye on the front entrance. Maybe he won't be looking over his shoulder."

Mid-afternoon, we rode onto the caprock. Behind us, the rolling plains looked like an undulating sea of grass and sage. Ahead, the country was flat as a board and had a reddish tinge. We rode a couple hours into the night and camped cold.

Tevis glanced at the stars. "Where do you figure we are?"

I peered to the east. "Probably four, maybe five miles beyond the mouth of the canyon. I reckon we'll head due east in the morning, and then work our way up the canyon."

Over the millenniums, the canyons of the Panhandle have been formed by flash floods that ate away gaping fissures in the caprock, carving gorges two or three hundred feet deep into the rock.

Mid-morning, we spotted the canyon.

Without pausing on the rim, I headed north, searching for a route down into the mile-wide gorge. At this point, the canyon walls sloped to the bottom at a shallow enough angle for our horses to manage. I found a narrow cut, and headed down.

Gramma and buffalo grass grew in patches along the canyon walls. Shallow gullies cut by the runoff from rain and snow wound down the slopes. Between the gullies, clumps of berry vines dotted the slopes like cowpies in a barnyard. Back to the south, the walls grew steeper as the canyon narrowed.

We pulled up at noon and found a motte of scrub oak near a pool of water. Willows surrounded the pool, and animal signs were plentiful in the sand around the water. It was stagnant around the edges, but good enough for our horses.

"Why are we stopping?" Danny asked.

"This is as good a place as any. I'll go out on foot and try to spot the cabin."

Tevis nodded and dismounted, but Danny protested. "I want to help. I can look for the cabin too."

I shook my head. "You stay here with Tevis. If we have to skedaddle, I don't want to have to go looking for you."

He clenched his jaw. "That isn't fair."

His retort surprised me, but I brushed it off. "Sorry."

"It still isn't fair," he replied, his tone petulant.

They say patience is a virtue, but sometimes I reckon virtue can be pushed too far. And I was tired, worried, and halfway scared. I dismounted and loosened the cinch on my saddle. "Fair has nothing to do with it. You're staying here, and that's all there is to it."

"But—"

I spun on him. "Blast it, boy. I'm not arguing it with you. You will stay here with Tevis, and you will stop griping, and stop being so bullheaded, or I'll saddle us all up and take you back to the ranch and come back by myself. You hear me?"

He tried to stare me down, but after a few moments, he dropped his gaze to the ground. "Yes, sir."

Dismounting, I handed him the reins. "Now, stake our ponies out to graze."

While he did as I instructed, I eased to the edge of the scrub oak and studied the canyon to the south. The walls grew steeper. Patches of gnarled scrub and thin grass dotted the red slopes. I looked over my shoulder at Tevis and Danny. "I'm going ahead on foot, but I got a feeling we're still a mile or so from their hangout."

Tevis wiped at his wrinkled forehead with his bony fingers. "What makes you think that?"

"No fence to hold the stock, and the slopes. A cow could walk right up either side here. Farther south, the canyon walls are steeper. That's where we'll find the fence."

I was right. An hour later, I peered over the ridge of a wash and spotted the wood rail fence spanning the floor of the canyon half-a-mile distant. I studied the slopes, searching for the cabin.

Dusk comes early in the canyons, and even now, the shadow cast by the west rim was creeping up the east wall. Directly overhead, the sky was still bright and clear.

A rumble of thunder rolled down the canyon. I looked up, but all I could see was blue skies. Moments later, a breeze cooled my face followed by another round of thunder. I wondered if the rustlers were holding any stock in the canyon.

Darting from bush to bush, I eased nearer the fence, taking what cover I could behind the clumps of berry bushes or patches of box elders. The wind blew harder, picking up sand and flinging it into my face.

Another rumble of thunder rolled down the canyon. I glanced south and spotted a thick row of dark clouds sweep over the horizon.

I hurried back to our camp. A light rain had started falling by the time I arrived. Tevis and Danny were moving the last of our gear under a lean-to they had erected between a few scrawny elms on a small shelf about halfway up the slope.

The rain grew harder. Tevis gestured to the shelter.

"Didn't know how hard the rain would be. From the looks around here, flash floods are purty common. Reckoned on getting us out of the way."

Danny looked up at me hopefully. "You find the cabin?"

"No. Found the fence though, about two miles up. If the rain lets up, and we get some starlight, I'll scout around some more tonight."

They had rigged our tarps to form a two-sided lean-to against the weather. The shelf angled so that the water sluiced down the slope, leaving us as comfortable and dry as we could expect.

After a hot supper of bacon and coffee, I lay back on my saddle. The rain fell steadily.

Danny sat forward and wrapped his arms about his knees. He looked at me. "What if it don't stop raining?"

"Huh?"

"I mean, you still going out to find the cabin?"

I looked out at the steady rain. "Let's just wait and see what happens. The rain makes the slopes mighty slippery. A jasper could bust a bone right easy. Besides, without some stars, this canyon will be so dark that even the rattlesnakes will stay in their holes."

His eyes filled with disappointment. "Oh." He lay back on his saddle and stared at the tarp overhead.

Around midnight, the rain slackened. Tevis awakened when I sat up. From the darkness, he said, "Something wrong?"

I peered up at the clouds. They were still thick. "Nope. Just seeing if there was a break in the storm. Reckon not." I looked at the faint red embers twinkling weakly in the complete darkness surrounding us. I lay back. "Might as well catch another wink or two."

The drizzle continued.

The sun rose behind drab, low clouds, their dark bellies filled with rain. It was the kind of day that horses like to stay in the barn and cowpokes prefer to hunker around the pot-bellied stove in the bunkhouse.

I rose at first light.

Tevis whispered from his soogan. "Going out?"

"Yep." I glanced at Danny who snored softly with his back to us. "Doubt if they'll be paying much attention on a morning like this."

He grunted. "They might not even figured out we're coming."

I tugged my hat down on my head. "Don't bet on it. Meechum knows we're coming. Let's just hope he doesn't figure out when."

"Watch yourself." He nodded to the water rushing down the canyon floor. "There's a heap of water down below."

I grunted. The sound of rushing water had battered against my ears all night. Best I could make out in the poor light, the runoff covered about half the canyon floor. I doubted if it were deep, but any runoff in a canyon this size was swift—swift enough to knock an unsuspecting jasper off his feet. "I'll be back when I get back."

I made my way down the slippery slope to the canyon floor, then turned south, moving rapidly. Thirty minutes later, I reached the fence. Pausing behind a clump of spindly elm, I studied the canyon. Nothing moved.

Climbing over a rail, I continued.

The drizzle fell steadily.

Twenty minutes later, I jerked to a halt. I sniffed the air again. Wood smoke! The canyon was growing narrower, the walls steeper, acting like a funnel.

A grim smile played over my lips. They were up there, somewhere. And it was my job to find them before they learned I was around.

A half-mile farther I spotted the cabin, nestled on a shelf about a third of the way up the canyon wall. An uneven square of cowhide covered the window in an effort to keep out the rain. A natural slope led up to the cabin. A stick corral with a few horses took up the remainder of the clearing.

I started forward, then froze. Two riders appeared at the base of the slope. I dropped to my knees behind a clump of berry briars. Halliburton and Meechum. Coming to spell young Bud Tunney.

Water dripped from the brim of my hat as I studied the riders. Three-to-one odds were no good. I was fast with a sixgun, but not that fast. Besides, there was

Jenny and Emmabelle to think about. Stray slugs would be buzzing around like a swarm of bees. The risk was too great.

I backtracked, deciding to retire to our camp and plan our next step.

Tevis was standing beside our lean-to when he spotted me. He waved frantically and stumbled down the slope to meet me. "Lordy, am I glad to see you."

I had a bad feeling. I looked around. "Where's Danny?"

"That's why I'm glad you got back. I'm worried sick."

"Where is he?"

"He sulked around here after he woke up this morning, griping about how you wouldn't let him help none. About an hour ago, he got it in that hard head of his to go find Jenny and Emmabelle."

I let loose with a string of curses that even made my pony look around. "Why didn't you stop him?"

He looked at me as if I had taken leave of my senses. "Me with a gimpy leg? Why, that boy could run a mile and back before I could make half-a-dozen steps."

I waved my hand in apology. "Yep, you're right, but when I get hold of that little button, I'll jerk a knot in his tail so he won't be able to ride a horse for a week."

"You find the cabin?"

"On the east wall. A trail leads right up to it."

"So what do we do? They catch the boy, they'll know we're around."

I looked back over my shoulder in the direction of the cabin. The incessant drizzle drew a gray curtain over the canyon. "Here's what I got in mind. You're going to have to do some hard, fast riding. Think you can get your horse up the slope to the rim?"

Tevis studied the rain-soaked incline to the canyon rim. "Mighty slick."

"Well? We got no time to waste."

He grinned at me. "Don't worry none about me. What you got in mind?"

I told him as we headed back up to our camp.

"You're taking our gear. Roll it up. If I manage to get Jenny and Emmabelle out, we'll need it. If I don't, well . . ."

Chapter Fifteen

My plan was simple. I'd hide near the cabin. When Tevis reached the mouth of the canyon, he'd empty his revolver in the air. If we were lucky, the gunfire would draw a couple of them away, giving me time to take care of the one remaining.

Like I said, simple—like me.

Anyone other than a simpleton could have guessed Danny would pull some kind of wild-haired stunt. Now, we had not only the girls to worry about, we had Danny. I crossed my fingers he wouldn't give us away.

I shook my head as I watched Tevis top out on the rim of the rain-soaked canyon. Time for me to move. Tevis would start the party in two hours. I glanced up the canyon. I had to be in place.

The swift waters rushing down the canyon spread farther across the canyon floor.

All the while I made my way up the canyon, I kept my eyes open for that mule-stubborn youngster. I couldn't help admiring his pluck, but he had the Devil's own sense of timing.

Sometime later, I crouched behind a gnarled elm growing out of the side of the canyon wall and studied the cabin some quarter-of-a-mile distant. Smoke drifted up from the chimney and several horses milled about in the stick corral.

I didn't know for sure, but I had the feeling time was growing short. I needed to be closer to the cabin when Tevis did his part. I climbed higher up the wall. The slopes were slippery, so I had to move slowly.

Gradually, I made my way up above the cabin, out of sight from any eyes that might peer out the hide-covered window. No sooner had I squatted behind a clump of underbrush than six shots echoed down the canyon. Moments later, there were six more.

Below, Meechum, Halliburton, and Bud Tunney rushed from the cabin and peered toward the mouth of the canyon. I was too far to hear their conversation, but Meechum, visibly agitated, gestured wildly. He spoke to Tunney, then turned to Halliburton and jabbed his finger against the deputy's chest.

Tunney ran to the corral. Meechum followed. Moments later, the two rode down the slope in the rain and headed for the mouth of the cave. I remained crouched behind the underbrush, waiting for Halliburton to go back inside before I made a move.

Finally, he turned back to the cabin.

I slipped and skidded down the slope to the cabin and crept up to the window. I eased the cowhide aside and peered in. The interior of the cabin was as wet as the outside. Water dripped from the ceiling, canvas over sticks and covered with branches and dirt.

Jenny and Emmabelle crouched by the fire in the hearth, trying to dodge the water dripping from the ceiling. Halliburton sat on a log cot on the opposite side of the room from the door. He held a bottle of whiskey in his big paw.

Before I could decide how to get to him, the door burst open, and Danny charged in, Winchester in hand. "Don't move," he shouted, throwing the Winchester to his shoulder.

Halliburton did some throwing of his own—the whiskey bottle in a reflex move. The bottle struck the Winchester, knocking it aside. Before Danny could jerk it back, Halliburton tore it from the boy's hands and whacked a vicious backhand across Danny's cheek.

Jenny and Emmabelle screamed and rushed to the fallen boy.

The brutish deputy pulled back his foot to kick at Danny, but Jenny dropped to her knees at her cousin's side. "Please, don't hurt him," she cried. "He's just a boy."

Halliburton snarled down at the trembling trio for several seconds. With a grunt, he stomped over to the fire and glared back at them.

I couldn't go through the front door. The three of them were blocking it. If I shot Halliburton, Meecham and Tunney would hear. I glanced at the ceiling over the deputy's head. Maybe.

Before I could talk myself out of it, I scrambled back up the canyon wall overlooking the cabin fifteen feet directly below. I measured the distance to the stovepipe chimney belching smoke. Halliburton should be directly in front of the chimney.

I checked my Colt. When I hit, I wanted to be ready to fire if I had to.

I tried not to think of everything that could go wrong. If I stopped to think, I'd realize this was probably one of the dumber stunts I had ever pulled, yet in the state of mind I was in, I saw no other choice.

"Here goes," I muttered, drawing a deep breath and leaping feet first. I windmilled my arms in an effort to keep my balance.

A hundred and seventy pounds slamming into a canvas and stick ceiling will do a heap of damage. I did. Three quarters of the ceiling collapsed, muffling Halliburton's bellowing curses of surprise. Across the cabin, Jenny and the kids screamed.

I hit right on top of Halliburton, for I could feel him squirming under me. Then I smelled smoke. I glanced over my shoulder and saw that the canvas had fallen across the burning logs in the fireplace.

I jumped to my feet, and as the deputy struggled to his, I whopped him across the head with my sixgun. He collapsed under the canvas.

I stumbled across the tangle of broken sticks and torn canvas to the front door. I grabbed the end of the canvas and lifted it.

The three of them stared up at me, eyes wide in surprise. I threw the canvas back and opened the door. "Quick. Get the horses. We've got to get out of here before Meechum gets back." I glared at Danny. "And you, boy, I'll deal with you later."

While they bridled and saddled four horses, I pulled Halliburton from the burning cabin and tied him to a tree at the edge of the clearing.

He glared at me, his black eyes filled with hate. "I'll kill you for this, cowboy."

I nodded. "That's what Carstairs and Burgess thought."

His eyes grew wide then quickly narrowed.

Looking him squarely in the eye, I said, "Your time is up in Hidetown. I guarantee you that next time we meet, there will be a killing. It won't be me."

Halliburton trembled with rage. "I'll see you in Hades."

"Probably, but you won't put me there."

* * *

We rode north in the rain, halting at our deserted camp to pick up the coyote dun. I led the way to the rim of the canyon. I knew Meechum would follow us. We probably wouldn't be lucky enough for our signs to wash away, but I could always hope.

On the rim, we turned south, heading toward the Circle R. We had no supplies. Our camp on the Canadian River that night would be a cold one unless we ran across Tevis.

Someone must have been living right. An hour later, a solitary figure rose on the crest of a sandhill and waved his battered hat at us.

Danny, who hadn't said a word since we left the cabin, yelled, "Look! It's Tevis."

The old man gestured us to him. As we drew closer, he motioned for us to skirt the base of the sandhill. He clambered down to meet us, a grin wider than the Canadian River on his wrinkled face. "How you doing, Miss Jenny?" He looked up at her in concern.

She smiled wearily at him. "None the worse for wear. Wet, but that can't be helped."

He looked at me.

I nodded. "We're all fine. You see Meechum when he came out?"

"Nope. Never saw hide nor hair of none of them owlhoots. I been hiding right here." He gestured to the east, to the shallow valley stretching to the horizon.

"You can see for a couple miles here. If they'd gone by, I'd seen them."

"What do you suppose happened?" Jenny asked, looking up at me, her brown hair soaked and hanging in strands down her face.

"Probably they reached the mouth of the canyon, didn't spot anything, and turned back." I nodded to Tevis. "Mount up. We'll cut southwest. I know a snug camp on the Canadian River. Tomorrow, I'll ride on in to the Circle R."

"You? What about us?" Jenny said.

Danny started to open his mouth, but when I cut my eyes at him, he clamped it shut. I looked back to Jenny. "You're staying on the Canadian with Tevis until I find out just what's going on. I'll be back to-morrow night sometime."

The drizzle continued through the night, but within the ring of cottonwood near the river, we were snug in our lean-to. Our grub was plain, but hot. What more could we ask?

After the others slept, I sat at the edge of the lean-to keeping an eye out about us. I didn't expect any trouble, but it wouldn't hurt to see it coming if it did.

A soft voice behind me caused me to jump. "Cof-fee?"

I looked around. Jenny held out a cup of steaming coffee. "Thought it might take off the chill of the rain," she said.

"Thanks." I sipped it and shivered as the warmth of the liquid spread through me. "It does hit the spot."

She sat near me and stared into the night. Neither of us spoke for several moments until she finally whispered, "I want to thank you for helping us. Not many men in Hidetown would do what you did."

I was glad for the dark so she couldn't see how my cheeks burned from her praise. "Well, it wasn't just you folks, Miss Jenny. We are all tangled up in this mess together."

"I know, but you could have left the state, left it all behind. But you didn't. You stayed. That's what I meant about not many men doing."

A strange impulse seemed to settle on me, the impulse to talk to her about things I always considered personal and private. I sensed she would understand.

"Maybe, maybe not. I don't know why, but I finally decided I wasn't going to run any more. You see, from the time my pa was murdered by scavengers, I've been running. I found them, those that killed Pa, and I paid them back, but I ran from that, from the law. I ran into the war. When it was over, I kept running. Every time I saw a familiar face, I figured the law would be after me again. When Meechum framed me with Obery Phillips's murder, I realized it was his kind that kept me on the run, but only because I let them do it. Somewhere, sometime, a man has to take a stand."

She shook her head. In the dim glow of the dying

fire, I saw both sympathy and pain in her face. "I'm sorry."

With a chuckle, I continued. "Don't misunderstand. I'm not too swift. I didn't figure all that out when they threw me in jail, I mean about letting his kind keep me on the run. It all came to me like little pieces of a puzzle over the next few days until finally it all made sense. So now, I couldn't run if I wanted to. This is one poker game that I'll stay in until every card is turned up."

She nodded. "Sounds like my pa," she whispered, staring at the damp ground in front of her where she was drawing circles in the sand. "He wouldn't back off from anything. When that last Comanche war party came through, he insisted on fighting them off. Ma hid me under the floor of the house and fought at his side. At least," she added, tears brimming her eyes, "that's how I found them when I came up. They were side by side."

She looked up at me. "That was six years ago. And for the first time since, I think I understand what my pa was trying to say."

It was my turn to say "I'm sorry."

She smiled faintly at me and stifled a yawn.

I grinned. "Best you get some sleep. Morning'll be here soon."

With the sun, I rode out, heading directly for the Circle R. I didn't know what to expect when I got

there, but one fact was certain, I would ride in ready
for trouble.

Mid-afternoon, I reined up and studied the silent
ranch to the south. No horses were in the corrals, no
cattle milled about. The place appeared deserted.

A thousand thoughts ran through my head; foremost
was that Meechum had made one last roundup of stolen stock and was leaving the country. "Don't be an
idiot," I mumbled. "Why would he leave the country?"

I tried to convince myself that he had found Carstairs and learned that Burgess had vanished. Now he
had lost Jenny and Emmabelle. Maybe he figured he
didn't have a hole card to play.

Regardless of how hard I tried, I couldn't bring myself to believe such a fabrication.

And I was right.

Leaving my horse in the sandhills east of the ranch,
I went in on foot, keeping the chuckhouse and bunkhouse between me and the main house. From the corner of the bunkhouse, I studied the main building. I
saw no movement. A few yards to my right was the
corral, which led to the barn. Less than fifty feet separated the barn and the main house, a distance I could
cover in less than five seconds.

First, I had to reach the barn.

Flexing my fingers about the butt of my Colt, I
sucked in a lungful of air and sprinted for the corral,
expecting at each step the jarring impact of a slug.

Nothing.

Only my labored breathing disturbed the silence of the ranch. Quickly circling the corral, I eased inside the barn and made my way through the shadows to the front doors. I peered through the crack between the doors. The main house sat silently, emanating a sense of complete abandonment.

"Don't move a muscle, cowboy."

The words froze me in my boots. My brain raced. What should I do? Leap aside? Spin? Break for the doors? I couldn't take a chance. I needed to buy some time.

The voice continued. "I told you I would see you in Hades."

Halliburton!

"Now, you'll get what I promised. Holster that six-gun and turn around, slow."

I didn't move. "Not even giving me a chance? That's what I figured you for, Halliburton."

He growled. "Shut up and do what I say. You want it in the back, I'll be plumb tickled to oblige. Now, holster that hogleg."

I slipped my revolver in the holster and turned to face him in the dim light. Slats of sunlight lay across the floor. Halliburton remained in the shadows of a stall.

I allowed my shoulders to slump. "What are you going to tell them, that you killed me in a fair fight? Or do they know you better than that?"

"Shut up, you blasted—" He stepped forward into the wedges of sunlight, then pulled back from the light. "I'll show you just—"

I heard the first click of his hammer.

I shucked my Colt and dropped to one knee, fanning the hammer three times. The barn exploded with gunfire, three shots as one. I rolled aside and back to one knee, my handgun still centered on Halliburton.

He staggered forward, staring at me, sunlight revealing the disbelief in his eyes. As the echoes of the gunfire faded away, I heard the second click of his hammer. He stood motionless, like a statue. Then his sixgun fell from his fingers, and he toppled forward, dead before he hit the ground.

Chapter Sixteen

Gun in hand, I searched the ranch. It was deserted. I peered across the prairie toward Hidetown. That was the only place Meechum could be, in his office or one of the saloons.

I dragged Halliburton out back of the ranch and buried him. I did it not so much out of respect for him—being dead—but I didn't cotton to the idea of Jenny and the kids coming back to a moldering corpse in the barn.

Afterward, I headed for Hidetown.

By the time I spotted the small village, the sun had slid below the rolling sandhills, lighting the sky with broad strokes of reddish gold and purple. I'd often

146

thought that had I possessed the talent, those would be the pictures I would paint.

For a few moments, I allowed myself to admire the beauty nature had in such abundance. I gazed about the vast prairie, feeling a strange kinship with its sweep and magnitude, a kinship I hadn't felt since I fled our home from the scavengers years earlier.

I shook myself from my reverie and kept riding, planning on slipping in on foot after dark.

The town was its usual riotous self, a street filled with curses, laughter, music, and drunks. I eased by the burned remains of the sheriff's outhouse and crouched in the shadows cast by his office. A dim light showed through the window.

Peering over the sill, I stiffened. I'd expected to see Meechum or Bud Tunney, but instead, snoring on the bunk was Frank Burgess. His busted leg had fresh bandages around it. Doc Spencer, I guessed.

I grunted. Some folks never learn.

The door opened and Bert Perkins stepped inside and looked around. He spotted the snoring deputy and hurried to him. "Frank. Wake up. Where's Meechum?"

"Huh? What?" Burgess struggled to sit up. "What's wrong?"

"You seen the sheriff?"

Burgess sat on the edge of the bunk, his broken leg straight as a branding iron. He ran his fingers through his red hair. "Nope. Not in a couple days. What do you need him for?"

Perkins frowned. "Not for a couple days? Why, I saw him coming down the stairs at the hotel yesterday. You ain't seen him?"

Burgess looked up. "The hotel? Yesterday?" He shook his head, puzzled. "I been here for two days. He never came in here."

"That's strange." Perkins scratched the back of his head, tipping the brim of his hat over his eyes.

"What was he doing at the hotel?"

The liveryman shrugged. "I reckon he was up in his room."

The deputy stroked his chin a few moments. "That sure is a puzzlement. You certain it was him?"

Perkins snorted. "Of course it was him. I know Jack Meechum, and that was Jack Meechum."

"Oh, well, I reckon he'll be over here sooner or later. It's odd, him being in town and not coming by the office. Anyway, what was it you wanted him for?"

The rail-thin livery owner glanced over his shoulder. "I got word of a trail drive over to the west. Figured it might be a chance to pick up a few strays for the army boys."

The deputy stared at Perkins blankly. After a few moments, the livery owner's suggestion wormed its way into his brain. His eyes lit up. "Yeah. I see what you mean. I sure do see what you mean." He grabbed a tree branch he had fashioned into a crutch and struggled to his feet. He tugged his hat on. He laid his arm over Perkins's shoulder. "What do you say you and me run the sheriff down and have a drink on that, Bert?"

Well, it looked like someone had tossed a polecat in the henhouse. Greed, or maybe just stupidity, had turned Burgess back to Hidetown. I studied the situation. The unanswered questions multiplied. If Burgess hadn't seen Meechum, then where in the blazes was the sheriff? He'd been in town. Was he still here? And if he was, why hadn't he dropped by the office?

Halliburton had to have passed on word about Burgess and Carstairs. I'd truly expected to see Meechum back in Hidetown, but now Perkins had tossed me a bobcat in a bag.

The only question was, Do I open the bag?

My only answer was, Do I have a choice?

I stared into the empty room, fuming over the fool I'd let Burgess make of me. As I studied the inside of the jail, a glimmer of an idea came to mind. An unbidden grin leaped to my lips. Centipedes. Long, twisting, curling, clinging centipedes.

I remember Danny telling me about the centipedes under the Jackson house. Yes, sir, old Burgess was going to get the thrill of his worthless life.

Backing away from the jail, I hurried down the shadow-filled alley to Cletus Jackson's house. The windows were dark. I didn't know if his widow had remained in the house, or if she were staying with friends.

I muttered to myself as I knelt by the back porch and opened the door to the crawl space under the house. I muttered. "Just don't make no noise, Jace." I paused, glancing around. I needed a container. I didn't even consider using my hat to hold the creatures. It stayed on my head, tight. Nothing was falling down my collar. Sitting beside the back steps was a lard can filled with empty whiskey bottles.

Quickly, I removed them and crawled under the house. I closed the door behind me and struck a match.

My eyes bugged out.

Within arm's length, half-a-dozen black and red centipedes about six or eight inches long clung to the floor joists. Others scurried into the damp crack between the joist and the floor. I wondered if they bit. I shivered. I sure didn't want to find out.

I needed three hands—one to place the lard can under the centipede, one to hold a lighted match, and one to scoop the devilish-looking creature off the joist with the blade of my sheath knife.

I solved the problem by sticking a lighted match in the ground, inserting the blade between the little beast and the joist, then popping him down into the lard can. After quickly capturing over a dozen, I crawled hastily from under the house.

No wonder the house was dark. There was no way I would have slept in that house after seeing what was under it.

I shivered all the way back to the jail.

Once, I glanced at my sleeve. My heart almost stopped. A smaller version of those I'd caught was crawling on my cuff. I stifled a scream, but I jumped sideways six yards and slung my arm away from me as hard as I could. Right then, I was so scared, I don't think I would have minded if my arm had popped loose at the shoulder, just as long as I got that centipede off me.

I don't know where he ended up, but it wasn't on me. I hurried back to the jail.

It was deserted. I peered around the corner of the jail. The street was still busy, but I saw no sign of Burgess hobbling along on his one good leg.

I entered through the back door and slipped to the bunk. Pulling back the blanket, I dumped the squirming, twisting centipedes on the cot and dropped the blanket back on.

Then I lit a shuck out of there.

Burgess hadn't believed the promise I made him. Tonight, I was going to scare the bejeebies out of him. Next time I saw him, I'd kill him.

The night was clear and stars filled the night. I figured I could reach the Canadian by morning if I rode steadily. I eased around the side of the sandhill behind which I had tied my pony to the sage and froze.

I blinked. My horse had disappeared. Momentarily confused, I looked around, checking landmarks to be sure this was where I had left him. It was. His tracks were there, and beside them was a second set of tracks.

"Blast," I muttered, realizing some hombre had passed by and latched onto my horse.

There I stood, in the middle of the Texas prairie with no horse, and the only place I had to turn was where I could very likely be shot on sight.

But there was no choice.

I circled wide of town, planning on coming in behind the livery. I'd wait until everyone was asleep, steal a horse, and be out of town before anyone knew I was about. The plan was nice and simple, uncomplicated. I saw no reason it shouldn't work.

Unfortunately, I forgot that sometimes, for no reason, someone happens to be at the wrong place at the wrong time for the wrong reason, and the wrong thing takes place.

I ducked behind a sage several feet from the corral and studied the livery. Several ponies stood watching me. I remained motionless until they lost interest and turned back to the feed bag or water trough.

I peered into darkness, trying to pick out the calico I'd been riding when Meechum tossed me in the hoosegow. The gelding had been a gift from a warrior in a small band of Cheyenne, for pulling his boy from in front of a charging buffalo.

That had been a few years earlier when the Panhandle and Midwest were carpeted with bison. Most were gone by now, but I had the fortune to see a herd of those black-humped beasts that stretched from horizon to horizon, and took half a day to pass by.

The street still rocked with noise and celebration.

Staying in a crouch, I crept to the corral and then edged around it to the rear of the livery. I figured on climbing into the hayloft until early morning when sleep was the soundest, before making my move.

Just as I reached for the door beside the corral, it opened and the glow of lantern light blinded me momentarily.

"Hey. What's going on? Who are you sneaking in here?"

I didn't recognize the jasper. I shrugged and slurred my words. "Just looking for a place to spend the night."

He held up the lantern to get a good look at me. He said, "I know you! You're that—"

I knocked the lantern from his hand and bolted down the alley.

The bull lantern burst into flames. He cursed and stomped at the fire. "Help! Help!"

I did a little cursing of my own as I raced away. Someone would now probably connect me with the horse out on the prairie. They would figure out I was somewhere in town. And they were not about to rest easy until they had me dangling from the end of that empty loop out on the gallows.

As I expected, a clamor arose. I hid in the shadows by the saloon and listened as cowpokes charged down the street to the livery. Even Burgess hobbled past on his crutch.

Men shouted up and down the street, and Burgess's voice bellowed above them all. "Search the town. Look under every building. Find that jasper. We're going to have us a necktie party tonight."

Gleefully, every man in town got into the spirit of the hunt.

I grew desperate. I looked around and saw I was standing next to the Alhambra Saloon, the saloon where all my trouble had started.

But, maybe it could solve my trouble as well. I hurried to the rear and hastily mounted the stairs leading to the second-floor rear entrance. I clambered up on the porch rail and hoisted myself onto the flat roof. It creaked under me. Gingerly, I eased away from the edge and lay flat, trying to spread my weight.

I could hear talking and giggling below. About every thirty minutes or so, a new set of occupants entered the room.

For the next two hours, the search for me continued. Finally, around midnight, they gave up and returned to the saloons for another round of drinks.

I remained motionless.

Hidetown drifted into a drunken slumber.

Sometime later, terrified screams split the silence of the night. Instantly, the town awakened. Cowpokes stumbled drunkenly into the streets.

The screams continued, coming from the direction of the jail. I grinned. I couldn't resist crawling to the edge of the roof so I could get a bird's-eye view.

A dozen or so torches burned, casting the street in a feeble light. Moments later, Burgess came bouncing out of the jail on one leg without his crutch, screaming and waving his arms and slapping at himself like he had gone crazy.

He jumped on a horse and, still slapping and hollering, headed out of town. The horse shied. Burgess lost his balance and fell. His busted leg hung in the stirrup and the horse dragged him apiece.

Some jasper jumped in front of the horse to stop him, but the horse spun, swinging the deputy like a whip. His head whopped against a hitch rail post, busting open like a ripe watermelon.

The whole town converged on him. I knew from the sound his head made when it hit the post, he was deader'n dried rawhide. Someone later said a black and red centipede crawled out of the pocket of his vest.

With all the commotion below, I figured this was my time to skedaddle. I jumped to my feet and hurried across the roof to the rear of the saloon.

Without warning, the roof at my feet collapsed. I sucked in my breath as I dropped like a sack of corn seed, landing feet first on a bed in a dark room. There must have been folks in it, for there came a string of curses that would blister a preacher's ears.

They didn't last long, however, for the floor beneath the bed collapsed, sending us, bed and all, plummeting onto the faro table below. We hit in a tangle of arms, legs, sheets, and blankets.

I felt some bare skin, but jerked my hand away like I had been burned. A woman's voice cut loose with as impressive a string of invectives as I've ever heard. In fact, had she been in a contest for creative swearing, I'd have voted her first place.

But I didn't have time to wait around and congratulate anyone. Since most of the bar patrons and bartenders were out in the street, I managed to roll off the broken bed and scramble out the back door before anyone got a good look at me.

Back inside, the woman continued to scream and the cowpoke to cuss. I reached the livery. It was deserted.

I whistled. My calico trotted over. I grabbed a bridle and saddle and two minutes later, I was heading out of Hidetown by the back door.

Chapter Seventeen

The calico ate up the ground between me and the Canadian. The night was clear, and stars so thick there was hardly any space between them. I was still puzzled about Meechum. I halfway figured that maybe when Halliburton told him about Carstairs and Burgess, he had decided it was time to move on.

Yet, he had returned to Hidetown and then once again, vanished. But only after going up to his room. That is, if Bert Perkins was to be believed. And he'd said nothing about Bud Tunney.

So, what was in his room that made him return?

He wasn't carrying a bag when he left, or Perkins would have mentioned it. A slow grin played over my lips when I realized the answer. "But," I mumbled to

157

the calico, "he could have been carrying a money belt under his shirt."

My grin grew wider. It stood to reason, if he had decided to fog it out of the country, he would first take as much of his loot with him as he could carry.

But on the other hand, although I figured Meechum to be a coward, I couldn't believe he wouldn't stand and fight for the crooked empire he had put together. Still, maybe he didn't want to take any chances. Better to live and spend what you had than die trying for more.

I shook my head and settled back in my saddle. Trying to figure out an owlhoot like Meechum was like trying to rearrange a spiderweb. Every time you touched a strand, it fell apart.

My calico moved at a running walk, eating up about five or six miles an hour. I figured on reaching the Canadian River about sunup or thereabouts.

Just after sunrise, I spotted a line of green on the horizon. The Canadian! I reined up and studied the trees. A smart man never rode in without seeing what was waiting for him. Probably nothing, but Meechum's mysterious disappearance still puzzled me. I reckoned I'd sooner spend a few more hours in the saddle than get caught with my pants down.

Swinging east, I stayed below the sandhills, crossing the river three or four miles below the camp.

I continued my swing, until I figured I was due north of the camp.

I cut back toward the river, staying close to the base of the hills. Soon the river came into sight. I dismounted and crawled to the top of a hill where I could look down on the camp.

There was no movement in the camp below. No fire, no horses, no nothing. The hair on the back of my neck bristled. Something was wrong. I raced down the hill to my horse and slammed my spurs into its flanks.

The camp was deserted. The tarps hung motionless in the still air. A skillet was lying facedown in the sand, the coffeepot at the base of a cottonwood, and a bag of grub strewn down to the river. The coals at the bottom of piles of embers were warm. Twelve hours or so—maybe more, I guessed.

I studied the torn-up ground.

Two riders had come in fast from the east. One pulled up, the other circled the camp and drove off the horses.

My blood ran cold. I didn't have to guess the identity of the riders—Meechum and Tunney.

I knelt and studied the footprints. Best I could tell, when Meechum hit the camp, everyone bolted in different directions, except Emmabelle and Danny. Their small prints were side-by-side as they scrambled for the river.

Tevis's boot tracks led to a broad patch of thorny

plum bushes, five-feet high and so thick a jackrabbit would think twice before going in.

At the edge of the plum patch, blood stained the sand. The bushes were shoved aside, indicating the passage of a body. Tevis!

I stepped on some of the bushes, crushing them under my boot heel and peered into the shadows inside the patch. "Tevis! You in there? It's me, Jace Quinlan."

A faint moan drifted through the slender trunks of the plum bushes. I worked forward, pushing the bushes aside and stepping on them. Thorns poked through my shirt and my jeans, but I slowly wedged forward into the patch. "Tevis. Where are you?"

A groan sounded to my left. I looked around and spotted the old man's frail figure. There was a spread of blood on his side and on his leg.

His eyes were closed. I said, "Give me your hand? Can you?" Weakly, he struggled to extend his hand. I leaned forward and grasped it. "I got to get you out of here. Hold on."

He groaned when I pulled him to his feet. I bent at the waist and draped him over my shoulder. I headed back, clenching my teeth and barging through the thorns and briars.

I laid Tevis on the tarp. He was leaking blood something fierce. I tore off part of my shirt and patched the holes in him. He was lucky. They were bleeders, but they wouldn't kill him.

When I finished patching him up, I leaned forward. "Tevis. You hear me? It's Jace. Where are the others?"

His reply was garbled. I dipped some cold water from the river with my hat and gave him some to drink. He drifted off to sleep. I felt his heart. The beat was strong and steady. He was a tough old bird, and I reckoned he'd be fine if infection didn't set in.

I rose and stared down at him. "That's one. Now for the others." I followed Danny's and Emmabelle's tracks down to the water where they disappeared.

The river flowed smooth and quiet, and the sagebrush on the prairie beyond waved gently with the wind. I rode downriver along the riverbank, studying the sandy bed a few inches below the clear water, searching for any indication of the two youngsters.

"What's this?" I reined up and reached for a willow limb that hung over the water. The leaves had been stripped from it. Next to it was another limb, the broken tip still dangling from the limb.

My pulse raced. The kids had come this way. I peered downriver. Nothing, just the sandy, grass-covered banks. Where the blazes could those kids have disappeared to?

Then I spotted a pile of drift logs heaped against a high bluff overlooking a bend in the river. I rode into the water and hurried to it.

Even before I got there, a white face appeared among the logs. A hand waved frantically. "Jace! Jace!"

Danny and Emmabelle tumbled out of the drift logs and splashed awkwardly through the knee-deep water to me. I leaped from my saddle and grabbed them as they jumped up at me. "You kids okay?"

Emmabelle's eyes were red from crying. I lifted her and dried her eyes. "It's okay now. You're all right."

Danny blurted out. "It was the sheriff. Him and a deputy came in and run our horses off. Tevis shot at him. When the sheriff went after Tevis, Emmabelle and me made for the river."

"Jenny? What about Jenny?"

Danny grew silent. He shook his head. "I don't know."

Emmabelle started crying again.

Back at the camp, I built a fire, and while the kids gathered the grub and cleaned it off best they could in the river, I followed Jenny's signs.

My heart sank when I saw the horse tracks beside her tiny boot prints. And then the tracks vanished. Meechum had her. I followed his signs a short piece to where it mixed with the tracks of other ponies. From there, two sets of tracks headed west, one behind the other, the way a horse being led would follow. A third set trailed.

I stood alone on the crest of a sandhill studying the western horizon. I hoped he would keep her, not sell her off to a roving band of Comancheros. I wanted to believe that not even Jack Meechum could be so cruel.

The one glimmer of hope was his feeling for her. On the other hand, a jilted man might do anything out of revenge.

If he did keep her, would he follow the river to Atascosa, or head beyond the rolling sandhills to the Staked Plains, a flat, treeless land that offered no direction, no aid for a traveler?

I hoped Meechum wasn't taking Jenny out there. If there were any spot on this earth old Satan could call home, it was the Staked Plains.

As soon as I got Tevis and the kids back to the ranch, I'd follow.

Back in camp, we managed to scrounge enough used grounds for a couple sips of coffee, and enough grub to stop the growling in our bellies.

"Soon as we put ourselves around this, we're starting back," I said, checking Tevis's wounds again. He was lucky. Both slugs had passed through. At least, he wouldn't have to be cut on.

Danny jumped to his feet and pointed behind me. "Jace! Look out!"

I shucked my Colt and threw myself aside, rolling to one knee and cocking the hammer. I hesitated.

Eyes closed, Bud Tunney sat slumped forward astride his pony as it ambled into camp. I threw up my hand, and the horse shied.

The young deputy tumbled from the saddle.

He had a hole just below his right collarbone.

"Is he dead?" Emmabelle whispered.

"No. Bled a lot, but not dead."

"Bud!" I shook him gently. "What happened?"

He opened his pain-filled eyes. "I—I tried to stop Jack—he shot me. He—Jenny . . ." His voice trailed away.

I shook my head. Now, we were in a mess. Two shot-up cowpokes, two kids, two horses, and me jerking at the bit to get after Meechum and Jenny.

"Who—who is it?" Tevis had managed to raise himself on an elbow.

"Bud Tunney. Hole in the chest."

The old man grunted and lay back. He licked at his lips. "Sure could use some water."

Danny washed out the coffeepot and filled it with water. Tevis drank greedily. "Mighty good," he mumbled, dragging the back of his hand across his lips and lying back. "Mighty good. The kids, Jenny, they safe?"

"Danny and Emmabelle are fine. Meechum took Jenny."

Tevis cursed. "Get her back, Jace. Don't let him hurt her."

"I've got to get you back to the ranch. You lost a heap of blood."

He tried to laugh, but winced in pain.

Danny and Emmabelle were looking on. She whispered in a frail voice. "Don't die, Tevis."

He forced a grin. "I ain't dying, little one, just leaking blood." He ran the tip of his tongue over his dried lips. "You hear me, Jace? You got to get her back."

"Like I said, soon as I get you back to the ranch. We only got two horses, and counting Tunney, two of you are shot up. We'll load you up, put the kids with you, and I'll lead you in. Then I'll get on the trail." I grimaced. That would take another day and a half, giving Meechum over two days' start, but I didn't know what else to do.

"Bull," Tevis growled. "What about Bud here? He bad?"

"Like I said, a hole in the shoulder."

"Then neither of us is dying. Put them kids on Tunney's horse. They can go in and bring a buckboard back for us." I started to protest, but Tevis kept jabbering. "Leave us water and what grub there is. Give me Bud's sixgun. We'll be fine right here until they get back tomorrow. You hightail after Jenny."

I could have given that old codger a kiss on that wrinkled forehead of his. I looked at Danny and Emmabelle. "Can you do it?"

Danny gulped. He nodded, grim resolution in his eyes.

"Yes," Emmabelle whispered.

Chapter Eighteen

I readied the horses. The children had tied rags over their heads against the sun.

"You ready?"

Danny climbed in the saddle. "Don't worry, Jace. We'll make it."

I plopped Emmabelle on behind him. "I didn't see any stock at the ranch. You might have to use this buzzard bait for the buckboard," I said, laying my hand on the roan's rump. "You ought to get there sometime tonight."

Danny looked past me to Tevis. "We'll be back tomorrow. Don't worry."

The old man chuckled, then grimaced as a shaft of pain hit him. "I ain't worried. I sure wouldn't mind if

166

you brought along that bottle of Old Crow I got stuck away in my Sunday boots under my bunk."

The young boy—well, by now, Danny was a young man. The young man grinned. "I guarantee it."

And they rode out. I watched as they splashed across the river and headed south across the sagebrush prairie. A part of me was riding with them. A strange feeling, one I hadn't experienced in years.

I slipped my Colt from its holster and checked it as I turned back to Tevis. "I left you plenty water and all the grub." I looked up from spinning the cylinder, making sure the action was smooth. "Bacon's a little worse for wear, but it's something to gnaw on."

"Don't worry none. Just—" He grimaced and hunkered his shoulders against the pain. "Just get Jenny."

I nodded to Bud Tunney. "He going to be any trouble?"

Tevis held up the sixgun. "He is, I'll just whop him upside the head with this."

With a brief nod, I slid the Colt back in the holster and swung onto the calico. I headed west.

I hadn't voiced my concern over the Comancheros. I could see no sense in alarming Tevis and the children unnecessarily. Besides, I think I was really doing my best to convince myself there was nothing to worry about in regard to the Comancheros.

If that were the case, I wasn't very successful, for the dreaded possibility stayed on my mind constantly.

The sand was still firm from the rain, making my trailing a heap easier. Their gait indicated they were moving fast. I resisted the urge to race after them, instead keeping my calico pony in an easy running walk.

Atascosa was a hard two-day ride. I didn't know what shape Meechum's horses were in, but if he maintained his gait, the horses would break down before halfway.

The trail followed the river, from time to time cutting across a sweeping bend in the broad, smooth Canadian. Mid-afternoon, I noticed Meechum's ponies were shortening their gait. His horses were tiring.

I pulled up where the tracks led into the water, then a few feet upriver, back onto the bank. They'd stopped to water the horses. I studied the tracks on the shore. I wasn't a clever enough sign reader to determine how old the tracks were. I guessed fifteen, eighteen hours, for animal tracks criss-crossed some of the prints left by the two horses. Probably, Meechum and Jenny passed by here before dark the day before.

The setting sun slanted brilliantly into my eyes. I rode with my head down, the brim shading my eyes from the blinding rays, making it impossible to see what lay ahead.

That's how the two Comancheros got the drop on me.

Had it not been for the calico shying, the slug would have caught me right in the mouth. As it was, it gouged out a bloody trail along my cheek and tipped my earlobe. The report of the rifle echoed down the river, but I had already tumbled out of my saddle, shucking my sixgun as I fell. I rolled on my back next to a cottonwood and lay motionless, my gun hand outstretched in the direction of the ambush. I squinted my eyes, waiting for the bushwhacker to show himself.

Two figures emerged from the willows along the river. One was a Mexican with a big belly wrapped with a faded red sash. The smaller hombre was a dirt-encrusted gringo. One side of his face was a solid scar, twisting his thin lips into a permanent leer. They came side-by-side.

If I wouldn't have given myself away, I'd have shook my head at their ignorance. Coming in together, displaying no caution. There's an old Bible verse that says something like "Ask and you shall receive." Well, these two jaspers were just asking for what they were about to receive.

The little gringo looked up at the big Mexican and laughed. That's when I shot him in the knee, knocking his leg from under him and spinning him to the ground. His sixgun was a reddish-silver blur sailing through the air.

I moved the muzzle slightly to the Mexican's belly and fired. He staggered back, his eyes wide. He opened his mouth to scream, but no words came. I fired again, this time into his chest.

He tried to raise his own handgun, but his arm refused to move. He stood for several seconds staring at me in disbelief. Then his legs grew rubbery, and he sank to the ground.

I rolled behind the cottonwood before climbing to my feet. I studied the two. The Mexican appeared dead, but he still held a revolver in his hand. The gringo was sitting up, clutching his leg and blubbering like a baby.

When he heard me cock the hammer on my Colt, he looked around in alarm. "Don't. Please, don't. I'm hurt bad. I'm dying."

"You're not dying."

He grimaced and squeezed his knee. "Please, help me."

"Throw your compadre's gun away."

He shook his head. "I can't move. I can't reach it. It's too far. Please, help—"

I fired again, tearing up a clump of sand at his feet.

The gringo screamed and fell back.

"I was trying to knock the heel off your boot. Next time my shot might just go the other direction. Get the other knee."

He begged.

"Then grab your compadre's gun and throw it away, or I'll put you on crutches for the rest of your life."

Crying and whining, he dragged himself to the Mexican and threw the gun into the river.

I came out. I felt the blood dripping off my chin and onto my vest. "Now back away." When I was satisfied the Comanchero was dead, I turned my attention to the blubbering gringo.

He looked up, his eyes filled with pain. "Please. Help me."

The truth was, I wanted to shoot him between the eyes, but that wouldn't get me what I wanted. Besides, only trash like the gringo and the Mexican killed for pleasure.

"The only help you'll get from me is that I'll leave you a horse. But, if you don't tell me what I want to know, I won't even leave you a horse." I glanced around the rolling sandhills. "Your compadre here will bring in the wolves tonight. You with no gun, no horse . . . well, if you don't bleed to death first, I reckon you'll have to find a tree to climb, except you won't be able to do much climbing with two shot knees."

He turned a lighter shade of pale. He swallowed hard.

"A man and a woman come by here last night?"

He hesitated.

I cocked the .44.

"Wait, wait." The words tumbled out, one on top of the other. "Yes. Big man. Said he was a sheriff. Had a pretty little thing with him. Me and Felipe here, we tried to buy her, but he wouldn't sell. Claimed they was bound for Atascosa to git hitched."

Buy her! I clenched my teeth at the words, resisting the fierce urge to beat the piece of scum before me to a pulp. "When did they ride out?"

"This morning. Sunup. Honest. It's the truth."

I studied him a moment longer, then holstered my Colt, cleaned the blood off my face and vest, and climbed on my horse. I looked down at the Comanchero. "Your sixgun's over there on the riverbank. I'm taking your saddlegun and his horse. I won't bother yours."

Despite the close call, a fresh surge of hope filled my veins. She was alive and with Meechum.

Beyond the Comanchero camp of the night before, I found two sets of tracks heading straight for Atascosa, one set following the other.

I rode hard. When the calico showed signs of tiring, I switched to the Comanchero's large buckskin with the fancy saddle trimmed with silver.

Atascosa was older than Hidetown, although that signified little, for Hidetown was in its first year. Atascosa had been around a spell, the only spot claiming any sort of civilization this side of Santa Fe.

I swung around the village and came in from the west. After stabling both horses, I ambled out on the street. I had no definite plan, but I figured if Meechum were around, sooner or later, I'd spot him.

It happened sooner than I expected.

Night fell over the town. Pitch torches cast pale patches of yellow along the dirt street. I'd taken a spot on a bench in front of the gunsmith. Pulling my hat down over my eyes, I whittled and watched.

I hadn't put a handful of shavings on the ground when I spotted Meechum come out of the saloon and head for the three-story hotel. I watched to see if any lights came on in any of the darkened windows, but none did.

Five minutes later, he came back out, counting a stack of greenbacks he carried in his hand.

Suddenly, I had a plan.

As soon as he entered the saloon, I headed for the hotel. Maybe I could find out his room number.

I stopped at the counter. It was empty.

"Be right there," said a voice from across the lobby. An overweight man pushed back from a table beyond an arched doorway, taking a last bite of biscuit as he rose. He hurried to the front desk, wiping the crumbs from his lips with the back of his hand. He smiled broadly. "Yes, sir."

"I'm here to see Jack Meechum. What room's he in?"

Still smiling, he shook his head. "Mister Meechum's out. Over at the saloon playing poker."

"I see." I glanced up the stairs. "Nice little place you have here," I said innocently, looking at the dining room through the arched doorway.

"Oh, it ain't mine. I just manage it. But we try to keep it clean. We guarantee no bedbugs or lice."

I nodded in appreciation. "Reckon you stay full up."

"Naw. We still got some vacancies. You need a room? Three dollars. Four with sheets on the bed."

"Maybe later," I replied. "After I see Meechum, I'll have a better idea what to do."

"Like I said, he's over at the Red Bull Saloon playing poker."

"Thanks. I'll catch him over there."

The clerk returned to his meal.

I circled the hotel, trying to fix in my head which lights were on. At the rear of the hotel, I slipped in through the back door.

The stairs creaked under my weight as I slipped up to the second floor. Candles sputtered dimly in the hallways. I peered at the bottom of the closed doors, hoping to catch a glimmer of light from within.

Softly, I knocked on the first door. I didn't figure Jenny would be able to answer. The only way Meechum could keep her from running away was to tie and gag her. I grimaced, thinking of the frustration and anger she would be experiencing by being so helplessly bound.

I knocked again. A guttural voice responded. "What?"

"Sorry," I said to the door. "Wrong room."

Two doors down, I knocked again. A woman opened the door and stared at me. She wore a black lacy robe cinched in at the waist. "Do something for you, cowboy?"

My tongue got twisted around my eyeteeth. "Ah,

no. No, ma'am. I'm looking for a young woman. Brown hair." I held my hand even with my shoulders. "About this tall. She's with a—"

She finished my sentence for me. "With a big, rough-looking cowpoke. Got a beard?"

"Yes. That's her. Him, I mean."

She pointed two doors down across the hall. "That's where they are." She paused and gave me one of those looks where her eyes were half-closed. "You sure I won't do?"

I backed away. "Thanks. No, thanks, ma'am. Much obliged."

She laughed throatily and closed the door.

Quickly, I slipped over to the door she had pointed out and tried the knob. It turned, but the door was locked. I cursed under my breath and pulled out my sheath knife.

Those old doors fit so loosely in the jambs, they rattled in a light breeze, so I had no problem inserting the tip of the blade under the trim and popping the bolt free.

Tied to the four corners of the bed, Jenny jerked her head around and stared at me in terror, but as soon as she recognized me, her eyes filled with tears. I touched my fingers to my lips and quickly slashed her bonds.

I pulled the gag from her mouth, and she threw her arms around my neck, sobbing. "Oh, Jace. I was so scared. I didn't know what had happened. I—"

"Hush. You're all right." I hugged her, enjoying the soft feel of her body against mine. "You're all right." I lifted her from the bed.

She lost her balance momentarily. I grabbed her at the same time she grabbed hold of the open door. She looked into my face. "The kids. Are—"

"Later. Right now, we've got to get out of here. Meechum will be back—"

A raspy voice froze me. "Meechum is back."

Jenny gasped. I spun.

Jack Meechum stood in the open doorway. In his hand was a blue sixgun, the muzzle centered on my belly. He leered at us. "Well, well, well, if it ain't Jace Quinlan. To tell you the truth, I didn't figure you'd ever run us down. Too bad. All that sweat for a six-foot hole in the ground."

Down the hall, a door opened. A woman's voice called out. "You, cowboy. That other cowpoke find you?"

Meechum glanced in her direction.

Jenny slammed the door on the big man, knocking him backward.

Chapter Nineteen

I yanked open the door and charged, lowering my shoulder and catching Meechum in the belly, driving him back against the wall. His sixgun went skittering down the hall.

He grunted. "Why you—"

I jerked my head up and followed it with a right uppercut, catching him on the point of the chin. The back of his head banged off the wall.

With a growl, he lunged at me, swinging a roundhouse right that I ducked under. I pounded him in the belly with half-a-dozen sharp blows. It was like hitting the side of a brick building. I could feel the impact all the way up to my shoulders.

He swung a left that caught me on the ear, knocking me off balance and sending me tumbling to the floor.

I hit and rolled, just in time to avoid the boot heel he slammed into the floor. I bounced to my feet and threw a couple jabs, trying to hold him off.

Meechum just hunkered his shoulders and waded forward, swinging wild lefts and rights. I parried some, others got through. I managed a few good licks of my own, but not enough to stop him from pushing me back.

He was easy to hit, but hard to hurt. I split his forehead, the bridge of his nose, and his chin, but nothing seemed to faze him.

Then I caught him on the nose with an overhand right. He jerked to a halt and shook his head. His eyes blazed. He clenched his teeth. "Why you—"

As soon as he started forward, I feinted to my left, then ducked to my right and threw another overhand into the side of his head. The big man stumbled and fell back against the wall.

Before he could push his shoulders off the wall, I was on him like the proverbial duck on a junebug, slashing at his rock-hard body with vicious lefts and rights. He stumbled back onto the mezzanine overlooking the lobby.

A crowd gathered below. I could hear Jenny behind me somewhere, but I was a mite too busy to find her. Out of nowhere, one of Meechum's ham-sized fists banged off my forehead, exploding stars in my head and sending me tumbling back on my rump.

With a roar of triumph, Meechum rushed me, aiming to kick me senseless. I beat him to the punch, kicking him in the knees. He sprawled on the floor beside me.

The coppery taste of blood filled my mouth. One eye seemed blurred. His face was a mask of blood. We grabbed each other and rolled across the mezzanine to the stairs, all the while slamming our fists into each other's back.

We bounced down the stairs to the first landing.

I jerked away from Meechum and staggered to my feet. He was a second slower. Before he could straighten up, I summoned every ounce of strength I still possessed and hit him with a left hook followed by a crossing right, spinning him around and sending him crashing through the railing and balusters to a table below.

The table splintered, dumping the big man on the floor.

I leaped from the landing, planning on inserting a boot heel in each of the vermin's eyes, but he rolled aside. I crumpled to the floor when I landed.

When I looked up, Meechum, his face twisted in rage, stabbed at me with a broken baluster. I jerked aside, but he drove the wooden shard into my left shoulder.

For a moment, the pain paralyzed me. He dropped to his knees straddling my belly and yanked the baluster out, and started to stab me again.

I don't know where the strength came from, probably fear of death, but I crashed a knotted fist into the side of his head, sending him sprawling to the floor. I staggered to my feet and reached for a chair to smash over his head.

Hands grabbed me and pulled me back.

"Hold on there, cowboy," a gruff voice said.

Another voice shouted. "Let the marshal through."

I looked around, dazed and numb. Jenny reached my side and hugged me. "Oh, Jace." Her words choked off as tears rolled down her cheeks.

A well-dressed man pushed through the crowd. "What's going on here?"

Gasping for breath, I nodded to Meechum who was struggling to his feet. "He kidnapped this girl, killed one of her ranch hands, and wounded another."

Meechum shook his big head. "Ain't nothing to worry about, marshal. My name's Jack Meechum. I'm the sheriff of Hidetown. This old boy is wanted by the law for murder and rustling. That's his gal friend there. She'll say anything for him."

I grimaced at the pain in my left shoulder. I placed my hand over the wound to slow the bleeding. "He's lying, marshal. He's the one behind the rustling. Him and his boys rustled cattle and sold them to the army over at Fort Reedstrom. It was them that killed three ranchers and wiped out that army detail. Then they put the blame on me."

Meechum's eyes narrowed. "He'll say anything,

marshal. Trust me. He was the one who killed them, him and his men."

Jenny stepped forward. In a calm, collected voice, she said. "Marshal, Jack Meechum is a liar. He admitted to me he killed the soldiers and the ranchers."

The burly man's face blanched in astonishment at her bald-faced lie. He sputtered. "She—she—"

I spoke up. "I've got witnesses who heard one of his deputies admit the rustling and killing. And one of his deputies is his own nephew. I can prove I didn't do it, marshal. The time that Meechum there claims he saw me killing the patrol and ranchers, I was fifteen miles away with a knot the size of a hen's egg on my head where one of his men shot me."

"It's the truth," Jenny said. "We found his horse in the barn about three in the morning. We backtracked at sunrise and found him unconscious a couple miles from the house. What he said is true. We live fifteen or so miles from where the ambush took place."

Meechum took half a step backward, dragging his tongue over his split lips. His gaze darted about the room. He stammered. "They're lying, marshal. They're in this together."

The marshal studied Jack Meechum. "First off, I'm a federal marshal. The Atascosa sheriff's down to Austin for a spell. So, I reckon I'll just keep the two of you here until he gets back, or I can get to the bottom of things. I'll send a deputy over to Hidetown to see just what's going on."

Meechum shook his head. "Atascosa deputies got no jurisdiction over there."

The marshal grinned. "One of my deputies, Mister Meechum. A federal marshal. My deputies got jurisdiction anywhere they want to go. Besides, you'll be right comfortable in my jail. Why—"

Panic filled Meechum's eyes. Suddenly, he shoved the marshal back into us and bolted from the hotel. I grabbed the marshal's handgun and raced after the fleeing man.

I slid to a halt on the porch and squinted into the dimly-lit street. I spotted Meechum as he ducked into the livery. A wave of dizziness hit me as I started down the steps. I staggered against the hitching post and held on until my head stopped spinning.

Taking a deep breath, I hurried across the street, expecting him to come boiling out of the livery at any second on his pony.

I reached the door. Lantern light cast dancing shadows on the far wall. I ducked inside, pressing up against the wall in a patch of shadows until my eyes grew accustomed to the indistinct gloom in the livery.

The large stable was silent as a tomb. I slipped along the wall, my eyes searching the shadows for any movement, any silhouette.

My heart thudded against my chest. Warm blood plastered my shirt to my skin, and the perspiration pouring into the wound sharpened the pain. I paused, studying the pile of hay before me. A pitchfork hung on the wall beside the hay.

A raspy voice at my back froze me. "You rolled craps, Quinlan."

I stiffened.

"Drop that hogleg. Then turn around. I want you to see it coming."

When I got on Meechum's trail, I had made up my mind I would get him, even if it killed me. I could spin and fire. We'd both catch a lead plum that way. But I eyed the pitchfork. Tines up, it dangled on a nail.

"I said drop the hogleg."

I needed some time. "All right. But maybe we can talk this over."

"There ain't going to be no talking. Drop it. And turn around."

I extended my arm in the direction of the pitchfork. "Here goes." I dropped the revolver, and in the same motion grabbed the pitchfork, spun and hurled it at Meechum's chest.

He fired instinctively. The slug slammed into my side, knocking me back into the stack of hay.

Jack Meechum stood transfixed, staring with wide eyes at the pitchfork protruding from his chest. He parted his lips to speak, but all that came out was a dribble of blood from the side of his mouth. He gurgled once or twice, then dropped to his knees and slowly fell forward. The pitchfork handle slid along the ground until it jammed against the wall.

Meechum died on his knees, leaning forward on the rusty tines of the pitchfork.

Chapter Twenty

By the time I healed, the marshal's deputies had returned from Hidetown. Once word spread that Meechum was dead, witnesses came forward.

Tevis was adamant in his defense of my innocence of both the murders and the rustling.

Bud Tunney, Meechum's nephew, supported Tevis's deposition without admitting his part, which was fine with me. I'd always figured he had been more or less forced to ride with his uncle. This way, Bud could move out of the state, start over, and find a better way of life.

The final proof of my innocence was the U.S. Army's identification of Jack Meechum as John Morris, the man who sold the rustled cattle to them.

One of the federal deputies remained in Hidetown until a new sheriff could be elected.

Apparently, the familiar face I had spotted in Atascosa a few weeks earlier was not familiar after all. No one had reported me to the sheriff nor the federal marshal.

Had they, one of the law officers would have recognized my name, but neither did.

Maybe my past was now truly my past.

The marshal grinned up at Jenny and me as we mounted our horses in front of the livery and turned them east. "Looks like you folks are going to have some new neighbors. Word is that the army plans on building a fort near Hidetown next year. Fort Elliot."

I shook my head and tugged my hat on tight. "It's mighty large country out there."

He stepped back. "It is that. Now, you folks take care, you hear?"

"You bet," I replied, grinning at Jenny.

She looked at the marshal. "And if you ever pass by the Circle R, we'd be pleased for you to stop in for a visit."

We rode through the cool shade of the cottonwoods along the river for several minutes without speaking. I looked at her. "We?"

She smiled up at me and nodded. "We. Any arguments?"

I eased my pony next to hers and laid my hand on hers. "No, ma'am. Not one. Not a solitary one."